Whatever After

JUST DANCE

Read all the Whatever After books!

Whatever After

JUST DANCE

SARAH MLYNOWSKI

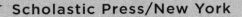

Scholastic Press/New York

Library of Congress Cataloging-in-Publication Data available

ISBN 978-1-338-77555-6

10 9 8 7 6 5 4 3 2 1   22 23 24 25 26

Printed in Italy   183

First edition, April 2022

for aimee friedman and laura dail,
team whatever after.
omg ten years!
thank you for everything.
xo with extra love and extra gratitude,
sarah

chapter one

The Fairy at Home

I can't wait for tomorrow," my best friend Frankie says.

It's Friday, and the school dismissal bell just rang. Frankie and I are heading down the hall with our other best friend, Robin.

Robin's other best friend, Penny (who is my *sometimes* friend), is walking with us, too.

"The school dance is going to be amazing," Frankie adds.

Robin nods, her strawberry-blond waves bouncing. "It really is."

Is it? I wonder.

Everyone around us in the hallway is talking about the dance, too. I get it. Our school dance sounds fun. Why?

1. It's only for fifth graders — that means us.
2. We can request our favorite songs from the DJ.
3. The gym will be decorated with streamers and balloons. Plus, there will be a refreshments table with punch and all kinds of cookies.

But here's why *I'm* not so excited about the dance:

1. I'm a terrible dancer.
2. I'm a terrible dancer.
3. Did I mention I'm a terrible dancer?

"I'm going to wear my gold dress," Penny announces, her eyes glittering. "And my new shoes."

Of course she got new shoes for the occasion.

"I'm going to wear my favorite off-the-shoulder sweater and leggings," Robin chimes in as we weave around a crowd of kids.

"I think I'll wear my jeans with the checkered pockets," Frankie says, pushing her red glasses up on her nose. "What about you, Abby?" she asks me.

"Oh, um . . ." I haven't thought about what to *wear*. I'm trying to get out of *going*.

Every time I think about the school dance, I think about THE INCIDENT.

It happened last month at my cousin Harry's bar mitzvah.

A bar mitzvah is a celebration for when a Jewish boy turns thirteen. It's super fun. There's a religious ceremony first, and then a party. With lots of dancing.

At the party, I ran onto the dance floor with all the other kids, including my little brother, Jonah. I didn't think twice about it. I could dance. Of course I could! I've taken dance classes. I've even made up dances with my friends. Dancing was easy, right?

Wrong.

I was moving to the music when I happened to turn my head, and I saw an older girl laughing behind me.

I moved my hand up, she moved her hand up. I moved my hand down, she moved her hand down.

Was she mimicking me?

Oh, wow. She was! And she was mocking me! Was I a bad dancer?

I took a step back, trying to get off the dance floor.

All of a sudden, I bumped hard into a different girl, who bumped into a boy, and we all fell like human dominoes.

The last boy fell into the refreshments table and toppled the cake, which was in the shape of an Oscar trophy because the theme of the bar mitzvah was the Academy Awards.

Yup. It was bad. Really bad.

The girl who had been mocking me was laughing so hard she was almost crying.

I was mortified. Everyone had seen what had happened. My parents and Jonah tried to make me feel better, but the damage was done.

Ever since THE INCIDENT, I decided that I'd *never ever* dance in public, or even private, again.

I definitely can't risk dancing at school in front of all my classmates.

No way.

"Abby?" Frankie asks me now as we head outside. "You didn't say what you're gonna wear. Are you okay?" Frankie is very thoughtful.

"Maybe she has nothing good to wear to the dance," Penny says, eyeing my orange T-shirt.

Penny is *not* very thoughtful.

"Of course she does," Robin says, sticking up for me. Robin is also very loyal. "And who cares what she wears? It's the dancing that's the important part!"

Exactly. "The thing is, I'm not sure if I can go to the dance at all," I say in a rush.

Robin's face falls. "Why not? We all have to go together!"

Frankie's face falls, too, and even Penny looks disappointed.

"There's stuff going on at home," I say. Which *is* actually true.

"Is everyone all right?" Frankie asks worriedly.

"Yeah," I say quickly. "Everyone is fine. We just have . . . a guest."

Which is also technically true.

"Who?" Robin asks, exchanging a confused look with Frankie. I usually tell the two of them everything, and I haven't mentioned any guests.

"Yeah, who?" Penny demands.

"Um, a friend of the family," I say. Which is not really true.

So what is the truth?

Well, I currently have a fairy living at my house.

Yes.

A fairy.

Her name is Maryrose, and she usually lives in the magic mirror in my basement.

Yup. I also have a magic mirror in my basement.

If I knock three times on the mirror at midnight, the glass starts hissing and then turns purple, and my brother and I can jump through the mirror, right into a fairy tale. We've been to fourteen different fairy tales, everything from *Cinderella* to *Little Red Riding Hood*.

Maryrose is the one who sends us into the fairy tales. She'd been trapped inside the mirror for a long time (cursed by an evil fairy!), but when Jonah recently cracked the mirror by accident, she got free and is now hiding out in my bedroom.

Ever since Maryrose escaped the mirror, she's been *very* weak. She's trying to figure out how to get back her full fairy powers. And I want to help.

"Well, I hope your parents let you come to the dance anyway," Robin says.

"Same," Frankie says.

Penny raises her eyebrows at me. I wonder if she suspects something. Penny, Robin, and Frankie have all gone into stories with me. But Robin and Frankie don't remember anything about what happened. Only Penny does. So I asked her to keep the whole thing a secret.

But I'm not going to tell Penny about Maryrose being in my house. Knowing Penny, she would want to come over and meet Maryrose, and I can't deal with that on top of everything else right now.

As soon as I get home from school, I rush upstairs to my room and close the door behind me.

"Maryrose?" I call out softly.

I'm still getting used to Maryrose being my roommate. I have SO many questions for her. Where is her home? Do fairies have friends? Is she going to send me and Jonah to more fairy tales? Or are we done now that she's been freed from the mirror? Do fairies like to dance? (Are they good at it?)

Because Maryrose is so weak, she isn't able to talk very much. Which is why I have all these questions and no answers. She spends most of her time napping inside my jewelry box. She can shrink down to a tiny size so she fits inside easily. It's very cool.

I'm happy to see that Maryrose is now sitting on my bed, and she's her usual size — a little taller than me. My adorable dog, Prince, is curled up beside her, his brown-and-white furry head on her knee. Aww. Prince loves Maryrose! He usually sleeps in Jonah's room, but ever since Maryrose arrived, Prince has been staying close to her.

"Hi, Abby," Maryrose says, her voice faint. "Thank you for the peanut butter and banana sandwich you left me for lunch. It was delicious."

"Of course," I say. I've been sneaking Maryrose extra food when I can. I'm hoping my parents won't notice anything is missing. Her favorite food by far has been peanut butter. She's already finished two jars of it. Yesterday, she ate it straight from the jar with a spoon.

At least I don't have to worry about my parents discovering a fairy in my room. Maryrose is able to sense who's coming. If my mom or dad is about to walk in my room, she shrinks and hides in my jewelry box.

I sit in a chair across from Maryrose, studying her. She has long wavy brown hair, pale skin, and violet eyes. And she looks . . . watery. Almost like she's melting. She sometimes flickers in and out of focus, depending on how tired she gets. I'm not sure how old she is — a hundred years old? Five hundred? A thousand? — but she looks a little younger than my mom. Thirtyish.

She's wearing a gauzy silver dress and silver leggings and silver pointy shoes. She doesn't have fairy wings. I'm not sure if she's supposed to or not.

Maryrose has a book on her lap. It's gold and very thick.

"What's that?" I ask.

"My fairy book," she responds. "It's five thousand pages long."

That's a lot of pages. I love to read, but there are limits.

"I've been reading it to find out how to strengthen my powers. So far, no luck." Maryrose sighs.

Prince lets out a doggie sigh. Maryrose smiles and reaches out to pet him, but her hand fades in and out. Prince is less freaked out by her wateriness than most dogs would be, I think. We got him from a fairy tale originally, so that's probably why. He comes with us into all the fairy tales now.

"I'm not sure why being on this side of the mirror has made me so weak," Maryrose says. "Otherwise, it feels good to be out. I was getting a bit of a neck cramp."

"How long were you in there?" I ask eagerly.

"Hard to say. At least a few hundred years. I . . ." Her mouth gets watery, which I know means she's too weak to talk more.

Knock-knock. Knock-knock. Knock-knock-knock.

That's Jonah's secret knock for when he wants me to know it's him.

"Come in!" I call.

Jonah rushes in and shuts the door. He sees Maryrose on my bed, and his face lights up.

"Hi, Maryrose!" he says.

She manages a little wave.

Jonah hurries over to Prince and scratches behind his ears. "Hey, Prince. You used to come running to me when I got home from school. What happened?"

"He's been hanging out with Maryrose," I say. "She might be his new favorite person!"

Jonah's smile wavers. "Oh. Well. I'm glad he likes her."

"I need to rest," Maryrose says through a yawn. "Going to sleep . . . in . . . box." She turns all watery, then shrinks down to the size of my pinkie and floats over to the jewelry box.

Prince lets out a bark, looking sad.

"She'll be back," I reassure my dog. "She's just napping."

Maryrose sleeps while I do my homework, and keeps sleeping all through dinnertime. We have spaghetti and meatballs, and I sneak some food into my napkin when no one is looking. After dinner, I go upstairs and leave the meal for Maryrose on my desk. I check to make sure she's still sleeping in the jewelry box and am glad to see she is. She looks almost pretend in there, like a magic plastic toy.

I say good night to my parents and Jonah, brush my teeth, and climb into bed. Prince curls up at the foot of my bed.

"Good night, Maryrose," I call to my jewelry box.

I hear the faintest snore, and I smile, falling asleep.

The next thing I know, someone is shaking my shoulder. I open my eyes. It's dark in my room. I glance at my alarm clock. It's 11:55 P.M.

Maryrose is standing beside my bed.

"Abby," Maryrose says. "I'm sorry to wake you up. But . . ."

"Is everything okay?" I ask.

"I need you to go into a fairy tale," she says. "Right now!"

chapter two

The Mission

"Wait. Why?" I ask, sitting up and rubbing my eyes.

"I was reading my book and eating spaghetti — thank you for that!" Maryrose says. "And I read about something that should restore my strength." She sits down on the corner of my bed beside a still-sleeping Prince.

"You did? What is it?"

"It's something that has healing properties for fairies," she explains.

Ooh, a special wand? Water from an enchanted lake? A fairy protein bar? I hope it's not something boring, like spinach. Although maybe that would be easier to find.

If only it were peanut butter.

"The crown ruby from the Kingdom of Douze," Maryrose says.

"Douze?" I have never heard of Douze. But I usually don't know the names of the kingdoms that the fairy tales take place in. "What story is that from?" I ask.

Maryrose tries to answer but her mouth gets watery again. She points at the clock. Which I take to mean, *You gotta hurry.* The mirror only works at midnight.

I jump out of bed.

"If you . . . need help . . ." Maryrose manages to say as she starts flickering out of view, "find . . . Minerta."

"Who's Minerta?" I ask.

"Fairy," she whispers. "Go now. The portal . . . is open."

She turns all watery and then disappears.

"Maryrose!" I cry. "Wait! Where did you go?"

What is a crown ruby? How will I know where to find it?

Prince wakes up and barks.

"Maryrose!" I call again.

She doesn't return — or respond.

There's no time to waste. I rush out of bed and change into jeans, a white T-shirt, my green hoodie, and sneakers. I grab my watch from my nightstand — it tells me what time it is back home — and strap it on.

"Come on, Prince," I say. He loves to go into fairy tales. And this one is extra important.

But Prince doesn't jump off my bed. Instead, he curls back up.

"Prince!" I say. "We have to move!" Unless he doesn't want to go into a fairy tale this time? I suddenly realize he might want to stay with Maryrose to look out for her. Aw. Who's a good boy?

I run into Jonah's room and wake him up.

My brother sits up with his usual bedhead. "I was having a dream about putting ketchup on apple pie. And it was delicious. That's gross, right?"

Jonah feels about ketchup the way Maryrose feels about peanut butter.

"We can discuss that later," I say. "Maryrose asked us to go into a fairy tale right now. To get her something that will give her back her powers."

His eyes widen and he leaps out of bed. I have never seen Jonah move this fast. Except when he's climbing a tree. Or skateboarding. Okay, fine, maybe he always moves this fast. He pulls on a hoodie over his favorite soccer pj's and stuffs his feet into his blue sneakers.

"Let's go!" I cry, and then realize I should probably not be so loud if we don't want to wake our parents.

Jonah starts to follow me out of his room, then stops. "Wait! Where's Prince?"

"Prince is staying here to keep Maryrose company," I say.

"But he always comes with us into fairy tales," he says with a frown.

"He wants to stay with her now," I say, pushing Jonah out the door. We don't have time to argue.

"But . . ."

"Jonah, we have to go!"

"Fine," he mutters as we rush past our parents' bedroom.

We hurry down the stairs, round the corner, then take the steps down to the basement.

Jonah and I run up to the mirror. It's as tall as I am and has a stone border decorated with fairy wings and wands. There's still the little crack in the glass that was there the last time.

Usually we have to knock three times on the mirror. But the glass is already hissing, purple, and starting to swirl.

"Whoa," Jonah says. "No knocking on the mirror. No Prince. This is all so different."

I grab Jonah's hand. "Maryrose said she opened the portal for us. Let's go!"

We jump through the hissing, swirling, purple haze.

Nothing different about that.

Thud!

I land on what feels like a very soft rug.

Oooh, we're inside somewhere. We rarely land inside. It's definitely more comfortable than landing on your butt in the middle of a forest.

"Where do you think we are?" Jonah whispers, standing up.

I get to my feet. We're in a big room. It's dark, but moonlight shines through the huge arched windows.

"Maybe a castle? It looks fancy." I point to the crystal chandelier on the ceiling.

"Look," Jonah says. On the wall is a tapestry, and KINGDOM OF DOUZE is written on it in fancy gold calligraphy. Underneath the words are three triangles and two squiggly lines — a royal crest.

Well, at least we're in the right place. We're in Douze,

just where Maryrose wanted us to go. But what fairy tale could this be?

I slowly turn around to get my bearings.

We're in a bedroom! There are six gold bunk beds against one wall. Each bed has a perfectly neat pink comforter and a pink pillow. Between each bunk is a gold bedside table. On each bedside table are two golden goblets.

Are there people sleeping in the beds?

Holding my breath, I sneak over to the first bunk bed. The bottom bunk is empty. I glance up at the top of the next bed. Empty.

They're all empty!

I wonder whose bedroom this is. And why they're not asleep in the middle of the night.

"I know where we are," Jonah whispers.

I turn to face him. "You do?" I ask. "Where?"

"The one with the orphans," he says proudly.

"What fairy tale has orphans?"

"You know! With the billionaire. And the dog. And the redhead. They had bunk beds!"

"*Annie?*" I ask.

"Yes! *Annie!*"

"Jonah, *Annie* is a play — and a movie. It's not a fairy tale."

"It might be," he huffs.

"I don't think the orphans in *Annie* had golden goblets on their bedside tables," I say.

"Maybe we're back in the story of *Snow White*," Jonah suggests. "And this is the dwarfs' room."

"Really?" We never go into the same fairy tale twice.

He shrugs. "It was just a guess." Then he frowns. "I wish Prince was here. I miss him."

I know. I miss Prince, too. I hope he and Maryrose are doing okay back in Smithville.

Suddenly, I hear a creaking sound below us. Jonah and I freeze.

Then we hear voices. And footsteps.

Wait. Are the noises coming from under my feet?

I look down at the soft pink carpet.

The voices are getting louder. People are laughing.

"Hide!" I cry to Jonah.

We go rushing under one of the beds. There's a chess set under there, but I push it aside. Then I peek through the slit in the pink-and-gold dust ruffle.

Creak!

"What was that?" Jonah whispers.

"I don't know," I whisper back.

At least we don't have to worry about Prince barking.

Suddenly, a square piece of the carpet lifts up. A girl's head pops out, and she looks around.

"All clear," she tells whoever else is with her.

It's a trapdoor. Right in the floor of this bedroom!

I watch in shock as girl after girl after girl emerges from the square opening in the floor. They're talking and laughing and wearing colorful, dazzling outfits. Sparkly jumpsuits. Leopard-print dresses. Polka-dot skirts. Shiny leggings and chiffon blouses. And they all have on identical patent-leather black shoes with little heels.

The last girl who comes out of the trapdoor is the tallest and looks like the oldest, maybe twenty-one years old. She's wearing a bright red dress. After hoisting herself up, she closes the trapdoor behind her and smooths down the carpet. "That was fun," she says.

"Wow," Jonah whispers. "How many girls are there?"

I quickly count them.

"Twelve!" I whisper back.

Each girl is slightly taller than the next, and they range in age from ten to about twenty-one. But they all look different from one another. Well, except for two of them, who must be twins. Some of the princesses have pale skin and some have brown skin. Some have long blond hair, while others have thick dark ringlets. And one has a short pixie cut.

One of the younger girls sits right on top of the bed we're under, her feet dangling off. Her shoes are all scuffed. She kicks off one shoe and then the other.

"My feet are killing me," she says.

"Mine too," says another girl, who is sitting on the floor and taking off *her* scuffed shoes. "I have a blister on my big toe again."

"My legs feel like cooked noodles," one of the younger girls says.

"So do mine," an older girl says. "But that was an awesome night of dancing."

"It really was," says another.

Dancing? Awesome? I doubt that.

After taking off their shoes, the girls head into what looks like a HUGE walk-in closet. When they come out, they're all wearing matching pink pajamas. Two by two, they all climb into their bunk beds.

The bed above me and Jonah dips down a bit as a girl gets into it. Eep.

Hmm. What story has twelve girls in it? Girls who live in a castle?

Maybe the girls are princesses.

Okay, so a story with princesses.

And dancing.

Oh! Dancing!

Could it be? It could!

"Jonah," I whisper. "I know what fairy tale we're in!"

"Me too!" he says.

And I say, "*The Twelve Dancing Princesses*!" just as he says, "*Peter Pan*!"

"Oh," Jonah says. "Yeah, yours makes more sense."

chapter three

The Snoring Prince

Jonah and I hold still under the bed, listening to the twelve princesses whisper and giggle in the dark room. I can't wait for them to fall asleep so we can sneak out of our hiding spot. My legs are starting to cramp. And I think Jonah has nodded off.

I was hoping all their dancing would make the princesses fall asleep fast, but apparently not. I have no idea what time it is at home now, or how much time we have left here in the fairy tale.

We need to find the crown ruby and get back to Maryrose.

Finally, finally, the princesses grow quiet. Then I hear a few little snores.

"Let me make sure they're all sleeping," I whisper. I slither out on my belly and peer around the room.

No movement. All the eyes I can see are closed. Some of the princesses are even wearing sleep masks.

"Come out," I whisper to Jonah.

He darts out on his stomach and stands up. I gesture to the door, hoping that it leads to someplace safe.

Jonah and I tiptoe across the room and slip out the door. We emerge into a small darkened hallway.

"What now?" Jonah whispers.

"Find the crown ruby," I whisper back. "For Maryrose."

Jonah scowls. "Why do we have to do what Maryrose says?" he grumbles.

I blink at him. What's his problem? Someone got up in the middle of the night on the wrong side of the bed.

"Because we said we'd help her," I remind him. "She's our friend. And it seems like she's getting weaker."

"Fine," Jonah says with a sigh. "What's a crown ruby, anyway? Is that in the original story?"

"I don't think so," I say. I'm trying to remember the story. Our nana read us all the fairy tales when we were little, and I always paid close attention. Jonah, not so much.

Suddenly, I hear a LOUD snore. And it isn't coming from

the princesses' bedroom. It sounds like it's coming from a few steps ahead of where Jonah and I are standing.

Jonah and I exchange a glance. Crumbs. Who else is in the hallway with us?

Walking on tiptoes, we nervously follow the sound — and stop.

The moonlight coming in through the castle windows shows a table and chair. A young man is seated in the chair with his head flopped to one side. He's totally asleep and snoring loudly. There's an empty cup on the table.

"Some guard," Jonah whispers. "Asleep on the job!"

Is he a guard, though?

I study him. The snoring guy has short dark hair, pale skin, and a patch on his fancy blazer, like a royal crest from a kingdom. The crest is made up of circles and squares; it looks different from the crest on the tapestry in the princesses' room.

Whoever this guy is, I don't think he's from Douze.

Jonah steps a bit closer.

"Careful," I whisper-yell. "Don't wake him! I think he's a prince."

"Prince? He followed us? Where?" Jonah looks around hopefully.

"No, not our Prince. A prince-prince. As in a royal prince."

"But why would a royal prince be sleeping in the hallway?" Jonah asks. "Wouldn't the king and queen give him his own room? What's he doing here?"

Just like that, the original story comes crashing back to me. I take Jonah's hand and lead him around the corner so we can talk in private and not wake the prince.

"I'll tell you the story of *The Twelve Dancing Princesses*," I begin in a low voice. "Once upon a time, a king had twelve daughters — twelve princesses."

"The girls we just saw," Jonah whispers. "Is there a queen?"

"I don't know," I say. A lot of fairy tales don't have queens. Poor moms. "Every morning, the twelve princesses come to their royal breakfast wearing shoes that are all scuffed, with the heels worn down. No matter how many new pairs the king gives them, the shoes are always worn down each morning."

"What are they doing all night? Walking on sandpaper?"

"They dance," I say. "The twelve *dancing* princesses, remember?"

"Oh, right. Where do they go dancing?" Jonah asks.

"I'll get to that," I say, waving a hand. "The king can't figure out how the princesses are wearing down their shoes every night. So he decides to hold a contest."

"Ooh, a dance contest?" Jonah asks. "Like that show *Dancing with the Stars*?"

"Not exactly. The king says that any prince who can figure out what the princesses are doing at night can choose whichever princess he wants to marry — and become heir to the throne."

"What if it's a young princess? Does she have to get married?" Jonah asks, frowning.

"I guess engaged to be married," I say.

"And the princesses don't have any say at all? That's awful," Jonah says. I nod. It really is. "Although I don't think *that* prince," Jonah adds, nodding in the direction of the sleeping guy, "has figured out anything."

"He hasn't," I say. "Well, he tried but failed. He sat right outside the princesses' room so he could see what they were doing. But the princesses wanted to keep their secret. So, last night, they put a sleeping potion in the prince's wine to make him get all sleepy. They waited till he was out cold and snoring, then they opened up the secret trapdoor in their room and snuck down the steps."

"We saw the trapdoor! Awesome-sauce! Where do the steps go?" Jonah asks, wide-eyed.

"Outside. To a riverbank. The princesses take boats to another castle where they dance the night away! And then they row back across the river, come up through their trapdoor, and go to bed. Which we just saw happen."

"Fun! But what happens in the morning?"

"The king looks at his daughters' shoes and sees that they're scuffed again. The king asks the prince how that happened. And of course the prince has no idea, since he was asleep and didn't see the princesses leave or come back."

"He totally lost the contest," Jonah says.

"Actually," I say, "he gets three nights to figure it out. Not sure what number night he's on now."

Jonah tiptoes around the corner and over to the prince. I follow. Jonah lifts up the prince's hand and waves to me. Thankfully, the prince is still out cold.

"Jonah!" I say. "Cut it out."

Jonah chuckles. "Sorry. But he's so deep asleep. What happens if he doesn't figure out the princesses' secret after three nights?" he asks, still waving the prince's hand.

"It's bad," I say. I make a throat-cutting motion.

"Yikes," Jonah says. He drops the prince's hand and

winces. "Is he the only prince who doesn't figure it out? What happens at the end of the story?"

"Lots of princes try to guess, but they all fail. Finally, an older soldier returning from battle comes across an old woman in the woods. He tells her he wishes he could be heir to a throne —"

"Who wouldn't want that?" Jonah says. "If you're heir to the throne, you can probably have ketchup with every meal if you want."

"True. And not just any ketchup. The fancy kind," I tell him.

"There's a fancy kind of ketchup?" he asks.

"Yes. I've seen it at Penny's house. It's in a glass jar."

"But what makes it fancy?"

"I don't know. More expensive tomatoes?" I am sorry I brought up the fancy ketchup. "Let me finish the story, 'kay?"

"But is it still red?"

"Yes! Focus, Jonah! So the soldier knows that every man who's tried to win the contest has lost his life. But the old woman tells him: 'Go to the castle. When you sit at the table outside the princesses' room, do not drink anything.' Then she gives him a cloak that will make him invisible so that he can follow the princesses and see where they go and what they do."

"Whoa!" Jonah says. "An invisibility cloak! Like in Harry Potter? That's amazing. So what happens to the soldier?"

"He enters the contest. That first night he sits down at the table outside the princesses' open bedroom door. A glass is there, full of wine. He *pretends* to drink it. And then he *pretends* to be asleep."

"Smart."

"With one eye open," I continue, "he sees the princesses get up from their beds. All twelve of them. He sees them open the trapdoor and go down the steps."

"When does he put on the invisibility cloak?" Jonah asks eagerly.

"Right after the last girl is down the steps. He hurries after them — totally invisible. He follows the princesses outside and gets in a boat. No one knows he's there. The twelve princesses row across the river to the dancing hall inside the other castle. They dance for hours. The soldier watches it all. He knows he'll need proof of where they've been. So he takes a few pieces of evidence: a silver branch from a tree, a goblet. When the princesses leave, he gets back in the boat, and he's quick to jump out first and rush inside the castle. He goes back to the table outside their bed-room and takes off the cloak so he can be seen. He pretends to be asleep when they come up through the trapdoor."

"Very smart," Jonah says.

I nod. "The princesses think they've gotten away with their scheme again. And the soldier does the same thing for the next two nights. And then on the third day, the king asks the solider to explain how the princesses' shoes got scuffed. The soldier tells what he saw, and shows the evidence. The princesses gasp. The king declares that the soldier may now choose his princess. The soldier chooses the oldest, and he becomes heir to the throne. The end."

"Wow," Jonah says. "Good for the soldier, I guess. Bad for the princess who has no choice about who she marries."

"Yeah, no kidding."

"But you don't think that's him?" Jonah asks, pointing to the sleeping guy.

"No. He's too young. And he's not wearing a soldier's uniform."

"Aw," Jonah says, looking sad.

"Yeah." I feel a lump in my throat. The sleeping prince looks so innocent!

"Maybe we should help him?" Jonah says. "So he . . . you know . . . doesn't die?"

I was just thinking that.

"It does seem like the right thing to do," I say. "But we need to focus on finding the crown ruby for Maryrose."

"Maybe doing one will help us with the other?" Jonah suggests. "We can find the crown ruby and use that to help the prince, too!" He pauses and adds, "What do you think Maryrose and *our* Prince are up to right now?"

Before I can answer, I notice the first hints of sunlight appearing through the castle windows.

"Speaking of *right now*, let's try to find the crown ruby," I whisper, grabbing Jonah's hand. "Quick, before anyone wakes up!"

chapter four

The Crown Ruby

We hurry past the sleeping prince down a long hallway that leads through the castle.

The walls are marble and there's a plush red carpet
underfoot. The ceilings are super high, with glass chan-
deliers dangling down. There are fancy gold sculptures
everywhere, but no sign of a ruby. Or a crown.

Thankfully, the castle is really quiet. Everyone must
still be sleeping.

"Do you see any crowns?" I ask Jonah as we walk. "Or
rubies?"

"Nope and nope," he says, glancing from side to side.

I spot something at the end of the hall: a massive clock.

We hurry toward it, and I check the time. 6:15 A.M. I glance at my watch. It's 12:15 A.M. at home. Hmmm. So it's six hours ahead here in Douze? Maybe. Sometimes time moves weirdly in fairy tales. I'll have to keep checking.

We need to be back home by 7:00 A.M. Smithville time. Tomorrow is Saturday, so our parents won't come and wake us up. But my parents are usually up and about by seven, and sometimes even working in the basement by seven thirty. We can't exactly pop through the mirror into the basement when they're right there, can we?

Jonah and I keep walking. We pass open doors that lead into empty bedrooms, all of them with ornate furniture and fluffy rugs. But no crowns or rubies. I wonder why the princesses all share one bedroom when there are extra bedrooms in the castle. Maybe they like it that way. If I had a sister, it *would* be fun to share a bedroom. Kind of like it's been fun sharing with Maryrose.

Anyway.

"Let's look inside there," Jonah whispers, pointing to another open doorway. Hopefully it doesn't lead into the king's bedroom.

We tiptoe into what must be the royal dining room. It's huge, with a long gold table at its center. There are twelve gold chairs, and a taller chair at the head of the table. On the wall hangs a framed painting, showing the twelve princesses and their parents. Ooh! In the portrait, the princesses all look much younger than they did when we saw them in their room. The youngest is just a baby. The king has blond hair, pale skin, blue eyes, and a serious expression. The queen has brown skin and dark brown eyes with dark ringlets twisted up in a bun. She's smiling. Both wear gold crowns. Neither has rubies in it.

I'm about to say we should try another room when Jonah pokes me. Hard.

"Abby!" he hisses, pointing to the far end of the dining room.

I look.

There's a tall glass display case. With something inside it.

A big gold cushion. And sitting on the cushion is . . . a crown!

The crown is silver and gold and studded with twelve small diamonds.

And right in the center of the crown is a ruby.

I stare at the ruby. It's big. About the size of a plum.

This must be it! The crown ruby! Woot woot! We did it!

We found exactly what Maryrose sent us here for. We are fairy tale geniuses.

"That jewel has to be the crown ruby," I tell Jonah.

He cocks his head. "How do you know for sure?"

"Because it's red," I explain. "Rubies are red, violets are blue? I know that rhyme and so must you?"

"I don't think that's how it goes," Jonah says. "But what do we do?"

"We figure out a way to get the crown out of the display case."

Jonah's eyes widen. "So . . . we're going to steal the crown?"

"I guess so," I say.

"And we're okay with that?"

I sigh, feeling uneasy. "Well, no. Of course it's not right to steal. But we need that ruby for Maryrose to get her powers back! Maybe she'll return it to Douze after she's strong again."

He frowns. "I don't like this."

"I don't like it, either, Jonah! I'm not pro stealing. But what else can we do?"

The sun is streaming through the windows now. We have to act fast. I hurry over to the display case, and Jonah follows. I gaze up. The case is tall. Very tall. Hmm.

"Jonah," I say. "Can you get on my shoulders? And see if there's a way to open the case?"

"Okay," Jonah huffs, although I can tell he thinks this will be fun.

"Careful," I say as I crouch down. Jonah sits on my shoulders, and I slowly stand up. Oof. I used to give Jonah piggyback rides when he was younger, but he's bigger now. The good news is, he can easily reach the crown this way.

Jonah reaches out and touches the glass case. I'm sure he's leaving fingerprints on it. Crumbs. Hopefully we can just grab the ruby and go back to Smithville before anyone even knows we were here.

"It's locked," he says.

"There's no way to open it?"

"No. Unless we break the glass."

"We are not doing that," I say. "You could hurt yourself! Badly."

Also, I'm pretty sure breaking glass will be loud. If no one's awake now, they will be after.

"There has to be another way," I say.

A loud chime echoes through the castle, making me jump. Jonah sways on my shoulders. The next thing I know, Jonah is falling toward the display case, elbows first.

"Jonah!" I cry, holding on to his legs.

His elbows smash right into the case.

I wince, waiting for the sound of breaking glass, and Jonah's scream of pain.

But neither comes.

"Ouch," he says, still on my shoulders. "I guess it's bullet-proof glass."

"Are your elbows bullets?"

"You know what I mean."

"Are you okay?" I ask, worried.

"I think so," he says, rubbing his elbows.

We hear voices outside the room. Uh-oh.

"We gotta go," I say, helping Jonah slide down and off my shoulders.

"Where?"

"I don't know," I say.

The voices are getting closer.

I glance toward the windows. I don't think we'll be able to open them in time to escape. But the windows are framed by long gold curtains.

"Come on," I tell Jonah, and I pull him toward the curtains one second before the twelve princesses enter the room.

chapter five

One, Two, Three . . .

From between the gold drapes, we watch the princesses take their seats at the table. While last night they wore an array of fun, sparkly outfits, now they are all wearing prim pink dresses with white collars and white tights. They all wear their hair in identical tight buns on top of their heads (well, except for the princess with the pixie cut). The only thing they have on that's the same from last night are their scuffed black patent-leather shoes.

The king enters the room, wearing a purple robe with the royal crest of Douze. He looks just like he did in the portrait, but older, his blond hair now streaked with gray. He takes his seat at the head of the table. There's no chair across from him. No queen. I was right. Poor fairy tale moms.

"Good morning, One, Two, Three, Four, Five, Six, Seven, Eight, Nine, Ten, Eleven, and Twelve!" the king bellows from his seat.

"Good morning, Father," the princesses reply in unison.

Jonah and I exchange a confused glance. That was weird. Was the king counting to make sure all the princesses are here or something?

The princesses are sitting up super straight. Super formal. Their napkins are on their laps.

"They remind me of the kids in the beginning of *The Sound of Music*," Jonah whispers to me. "Wait. Are you sure we're not in *The Sound of Music*?"

"Shhh," I whisper back. I see what he means, but *The Sound of Music* is not a fairy tale. In fact, it's based on a real story.

I notice there's a clock on the wall, right across from where we're hiding. It's 8:30 in the morning here in Douze. I check my watch. It's 12:30 A.M. at home. Which means that nine hours here is about one hour at home. So at least we have lots of time.

Two maids in gray uniforms wheel in a breakfast cart and start serving French toast, scrambled eggs, and donuts. Everything smells delicious. Mmm. I'm hungry. Jonah is practically drooling.

"Three," the king says.

Three? Three what? Is he asking for three donuts? That sounds like a good number to me.

The third girl on the left side of the table, who's probably about eighteen years old, looks up, her brown eyes wide. "Yes, Father?"

Wait. Her *name* is Three?

"Your napkin is not centered on your lap like a princess's napkin should be," the king says.

"Yes, Father," the princess answers, rearranging the napkin.

"One," the king says next.

The tallest princess — the oldest — looks at the king. "Yes, Father?"

"Your water goblet is a half inch too far to the right," he says, eyeing it. "Your dear mother, may she rest in peace, always liked a perfectly set table."

"Yes, Father," One says, and moves her goblet.

This is weird.

When the maids are done serving, they wheel the cart off to the side, with the platters of food uncovered in case anyone wants seconds. I can tell Jonah is wondering if he can dart over and snag some food without anyone seeing him. He better not.

Suddenly, I hear a tapping sound. *Tap, tap, tap, tap.* What is that?

"Twelve, is that you tapping your feet?" the king asks, scowling at the youngest princess at the table. She looks to be about my age.

The tapping sound stops. "Sorry, Father," Twelve says.

So I guess One is the oldest and Twelve is the youngest, and in between are Princesses Two through Eleven. I can't believe it.

"No tap dancing!" the king says. "You know my rule. Seven, what is my rule?"

A girl sitting in the middle of the table answers, "The only kind of dance that's allowed in Douze is ballet."

Only ballet? They're not allowed to do any other kind of dance?

Jonah nudges me. I know what he's thinking. First of

all, it's absolutely bonkers that the princesses are named numbers. And second, Jonah and I sometimes think *our* parents can be strict, but it's nothing compared to this king.

"Two?" the king asks, turning to the second-oldest princess.

"Yes, Father?" she answers, daintily setting down her fork.

Is he going to tell her that she's not sitting up straight enough?

"Tell me where you and your sisters go every night," he says.

Oh.

Two doesn't answer. Neither do any of the other princesses. They just eat their breakfast in silence.

The king sighs. "Okay, then. Bring in the prince!" he calls out. "Let's see what he knows!"

Jonah and I exchange a worried glance. The prince is not going to know anything.

A maid rushes out and returns with the young man we saw sleeping in the hall. He's wide-awake now, but his fancy blazer is rumpled and his dark hair is a bit disheveled.

"I present Prince Gene of Wexley," the maid says, then steps back.

The prince looks nervous. His hands are shaking. His dark eyes are darting around.

"Your report, Prince," the king says.

"Um, well, the thing is," Prince Gene begins.

The king frowns. Uh-oh.

I glance over at the princesses. Princess One has the slightest bit of a smile on her face.

Prince Gene clears his throat. "I did not see where the princesses went last night. It must be because they did not go anywhere and were in their beds all evening?"

The king lifts his chin. "One, Two, Three, Four, Five, Six, Seven, Eight, Nine, Ten, Eleven, Twelve?" he calls out.

"Yes, Father?" the princesses all say at the same time.

"Stick out your shoes so I can see them," he orders.

The girls turn in their chairs and stick out their feet. Their shoes are even more scuffed than I realized. The heels are worn down to nubs.

The king glares at the prince. "Obviously they went *somewhere*!" he barks. "They did *something* that ruined their shoes — again."

The princesses stare straight ahead. All without any expression.

"Five!" the king snaps. "Where did you and your sisters go

last night that caused your shoes to scuff this way?"

Princess Five turns to him. "We didn't go anywhere, Father."

The king scowls. "Well, Prince Gene. Last night was your first attempt at finding out the mystery of the scuffed shoes. You have two more nights."

The prince looks scared, but he nods. "Yes, King LaPear. I will not let you down."

"Two other princes before you have tried and failed," the king says snidely. "What makes you think you will be successful?"

"Because I am Prince Gene of Wexley, that's why!" the prince says, puffing out his chest. "Wexleyans do not fail!"

I see a few of the girls smirk.

I get it, but c'mon, princesses. It's off with this guy's head if he fails! And the sisters know it. How can they be smirky about this?

The poor prince. I mean, he has a job to do. Just like Jonah and I have a job to do. To get that crown ruby.

Although, we're going to get that ruby. And he's going to fail. We know he's going to fail. Unless we help him.

"Really, Father," Two says. "We didn't leave our room."

"Liar, liar, pants on fire," Jonah whispers.

The king sighs. "I will once again order the royal cob-
blers to make all of you new shoes this morning."

OMG, new shoes every single day? Penny would love
it here.

The king points at the prince. "And I would advise
you to spend the day working on your eye muscles, Prince
Gene," he says.

"My eye muscles?" the prince repeats. He looks
confused.

"Yes!" the king shouts. "Because tonight, you need to
keep those eyes open and watching. If you can tell me what
the princesses do to scuff their shoes, you can choose one
of my lovely daughters as your bride. And you will become
heir to the throne. Do you see that crown in the display?"
He motions to the crown. Our crown.

"Yes," the prince says.

"We call it the Ruby Crown. And as heir to the throne,
you can wear it immediately."

I nudge Jonah. He nudges me back.

The Ruby Crown. The crown ruby!

Prince Gene puffs out his chest again. "Will do, Your
Royal Majesty."

"Two more tries," the king says, holding up two fingers.

45

"Two days from now, right after the princesses' ballet recital at four P.M., is your deadline. Get it? *Dead*line."

The prince swallows hard. "Yes, King LaPear," he says, giving him a salute.

Yikes.

"And you must bring me *proof*," the king adds. "Proof of where the princesses have been going every night. After the ballet recital, we will gather here in the dining room. You will make your announcement, show your proof, and you can be engaged to a princess, to be wed on her twenty-first birthday. You can wear the Ruby Crown as my gift and promise that you shall someday be King of Douze."

"Got it, King LaPear!" the prince says.

Hmm. If the ballet recital is two days from now at 4:00 P.M., that means the prince's announcement will be due around 5:00 P.M. That will be about 6:45 A.M. Smithville time. Just in time for us to be going home.

I think about what to do. We need the ruby. But we can't let the prince get his head chopped off. That's just wrong.

King LaPear finishes his breakfast and leaves the room, the maids trailing him. The princesses line up in order of age and exit the room after him. Only Prince Gene stays behind, standing there awkwardly. He is using his fingers to stretch

46

his eyes up and down. Now he's making them wide and then squinting. Oh, brother. Is he doing eye exercises to help keep them open tonight?

Prince Gene doesn't seem very smart. He's not going to be much help to himself.

So how are we going to save him?

And Maryrose?

"Abby — " Jonah whispers.

"Shhh, I'm trying to think."

"But I have an idea."

"You do? What?"

"Well, last night, Prince Gene fell asleep because he drank whatever was in the wine that was put on his table," Jonah says. "Just like in the story, right?"

"Right," I confirm.

"So let's tell him not to drink the wine. We'll tell him to *pretend* to be asleep and then follow the princesses."

I stare at my kid brother. "That's not bad."

Jonah's little chest puffs out even more than the prince's did earlier. "He'll see where they go," Jonah says. "What they do. And he'll find some proof to bring back to show the king."

Which means: Prince Gene will win the contest. He'll get engaged to a princess. He'll get the Ruby Crown.

"One problem, though," I say.

"Ugh, I hate problems," Jonah responds.

"Prince Gene will get the crown. With the ruby that *we* need on it. Why would he give the ruby to us?"

Jonah bites his lip.

"Unless . . ." I say. "We tell him we know how he can win the contest. And in exchange for the information, he has to promise to give us the ruby from the crown."

Jonah's face lights up. "Yeah!"

I give Jonah a quiet high five.

Then I leap out from behind the curtain. Jonah jumps out, too.

"Ahh!" Prince Gene cries, stepping back. "Where did you two come from?"

"Sorry to scare you," I say. "I'm Abby, and this is my brother, Jonah. We're here to help you."

"Thank you," the prince says. "Um . . . with what?"

"We know how you can find out where the princesses go every night," I tell him.

The prince smiles. "Great!"

"It is," I say. "But if you want to win the contest, you'll have to give us something in exchange."

"Ah," he says. "A deal. What do you want?"

"The crown ruby," I say.

"The ruby?" he repeats. "Sure, I'll give you the ruby as a trade for helping me win the contest. If you want to know the truth . . . I didn't even want to enter," he admits. "My parents are making me. Douze is much richer than our kingdom, so my parents said I had to give it a shot."

"Even though you'll, um, die if you fail?" Jonah asks.

The prince pales. "Yeah. I guess they're hoping I'm gonna win."

Eep.

"But the trade sounds fair to me," the prince adds. "If I win, I'll get the *entire* kingdom. I don't need the ruby, too."

Jonah pumps his fist in the air. "Yes!"

"Promise?" I ask the prince.

He crosses his heart. "Promise."

"You should know that we have fairy magic on our side, and if you double-cross us . . ." I shake my head. "It's not good for you."

"I would never! I am a man of my word!"

I hope he's telling the truth. "Okay. So here's the thing. There was a cup on the table you were sitting at last night, right?" I ask.

"Yes," the prince answers. "Full of a sweet, delicious wine."

"That made you very sleepy," I point out.

He tilts his head. "Now that you mention it, yes. I fell asleep right after I drank it."

I wait for him to put two and two together. He doesn't.

"Prince Gene, do not drink the wine tonight," I tell him. "That way, you won't fall asleep."

He gasps and snaps his fingers. "I get it now! I will not drink the wine."

I breathe a sigh of relief.

"You should pretend to fall asleep, though," Jonah tells him.

Prince Gene scrunches his forehead. "Why?"

"Because," Jonah says, "then you'll put on your invisibility cloak and follow the princesses."

"I have an invisibility cloak?" the prince asks, brightening. "Rock on!"

Oh. Wait. "We forgot about the invisibility cloak part!" I say. Crumbs.

"So I *don't* have one?" asks the prince.

"No," I say. Crumbs, crumbs, crumbs. "At least not that I know of."

"So I should pretend to be invisible?" he asks. He closes

his eyes, puts out his arms zombie-like, and walks around the room.

Yowza. This guy. Not the smartest prince I've ever encountered. Sweet, though.

I turn to my brother. "Hmm. Small snag in the plan."

"Where did the soldier in the story get the cloak from again?" Jonah asks.

"Ouch!" cries the prince. He rubs his legs. He's bumped into the table.

"Are you okay?" I ask.

"Being invisible is harder than it looks," he says.

"You're not invisible just because your eyes are closed," Jonah says.

"*You* were invisible when my eyes were closed," the prince tells him.

Jonah and I look back at each other. "Anyway," I say. "An old woman gave him the cloak."

"An old woman with magical powers. Was it a fairy?" Jonah asks.

Oh! Wait!

"Minerta!" I exclaim. "I bet it's her! Maryrose said someone named Minerta would help us if we needed it."

"Perfect," Jonah says, "but how do we find her? We don't have a fairy Bat-Signal or anything."

"I guess we have to go looking for her," I say.

"Should I come with you?" Prince Gene asks.

"Um, why don't we go and you stay here?" I say. I'm worried he might slow us down. "Just don't tell anyone about our plan, okay?"

"Roger that," he says, saluting.

"We'll be back with the cloak as soon as possible," I tell him.

"I'm going to keep practicing being invisible," the prince says, then turns to leave the room.

"Don't get hurt!" I call after him.

"Maybe we should eat something before we go," Jonah says, eyeing the leftover platters of food. "You know, for strength."

"Good idea," I say, reaching for a donut.

Jonah stuffs a whole donut in his mouth. "Mmm. Strawberry filling!"

I'm about to tell him not to talk with his mouth full, when someone walks into the room.

And it's not Prince Gene.

It's one of the princesses.

chapter six

Fairy Power

It's Three, the third oldest. She's tall and slender, with light brown skin, brown eyes, and shiny brown hair pulled up in a bun.

"Hi," she says. "Who are you?"

I swallow the rest of my donut. "Um, I'm Abby, and this is Jonah." My heart is pounding. Is Three going to tell the king we're here? Are WE going to have our heads chopped off?

"Do you work in the palace?" she asks. "Are you new?"

"Yes!" I say, thinking fast. "We . . . work in the kitchen. We're . . . cooks." Very young cooks.

Jonah nods, his mouth too stuffed with donut to speak.

"Ooh," Three says, snagging a donut for herself. "Thanks for breakfast. These donuts are delicious."

Jonah swallows. "You're welcome," he says proudly, as if he actually made them.

"You're Three, right?" I ask the princess.

"Yup. But I call myself Terry."

"Is your real name Three, though?" Jonah asks.

Terry nods. "My dad named us by birth order."

"I guess that's better than naming you out of order," Jonah says.

Terry takes a bite of her donut. "I guess. Although it's still annoying. It's like he doesn't want us to be individuals. And can you believe he made any dancing besides ballet illegal in the Kingdom of Douze?"

"That is ridiculous," Jonah says.

I completely agree. Even if I don't want to do it (ever), that doesn't mean dancing should be illegal.

Terry huffs. "I don't even like ballet! I like gymnastics." She shrugs. "He just wants us to be good little princesses and marry us off when the time comes."

Ouch. "Not cool," I say.

"I know! I mean, I'm not opposed to getting married." Her cheeks redden and she gives a shy smile. "I might even have a little crush on someone. But it's a secret crush. So don't tell."

"I won't." Who would I even tell? "Terry," I say, looking past her to make sure no one is coming. "Do you know someone named Minerta?"

"The woman in the woods?"

"Maybe?"

Terry nods. "There's a woman named Minerta who lives in the woods. She's always collecting flower petals and twigs."

"That must be her. Would you be able to direct us to where she is?"

"No problem," Terry says. "Make a right out of this room, and take the side door at the end of the hall. Follow the stone walkway out of the castle. You'll come to the woods. There's a white pebbly path in the forest that leads to a little yellow hut. That's Minerta's house."

Perfect.

"But it's a long walk," Terry adds. "A few hours, at least."

"We can do it," I say. We just have to be back to give Prince Gene the invisibility cloak before the princesses leave for the night.

"Well, gotta go. It's time for school," Terry says with a roll of her eyes.

"Where's your school?" Jonah asks.

"In the castle." Terry sighs. "That's where our ballet lessons are, too. And our ballet recitals. Everything we do is in the castle."

Except for your secret night dancing! I think, but don't say.

Terry turns to go. "See ya later!"

"Bye, and thanks!" I call after her.

"She's nice," Jonah says.

She really is. "Let's go find Minerta," I tell him.

Instead of rushing to the door, Jonah selects another donut. Like we have all the time in the world. Which we don't.

"Jonah. Terry said it's a long walk to Minerta's hut."

He shrugs.

"Jonah, what's going on? What's wrong?"

"Nothing." He shrugs again. "Fine. Let's go."

We walk to the doorway and look to the left and the right.

"No one is coming," I whisper. "Let's move."

We head for the door at the end of the hall. I turn the handle, and we slip outside. We did it! Woot woot. We are so good at sneaking around, even without an invisibility cloak.

The outside of the castle is made of glittering, light gray

stones. The grounds are manicured, with perfect green grass and pink flowers. Pretty! And the stone walkway up ahead leads to —

"There." I point across the castle grounds. "The woods!"

We go running into the woods. The trees are in neat rows. Like the castle, and the princesses, everything in Douze seems tidy and orderly. It's nice, but I could see how it might feel like TOO much tidiness.

Jonah and I walk and walk and walk. Terry *did* say it would be a while.

"Too bad we don't have your skateboard," I tell Jonah. "That would make us go slightly faster."

Jonah sighs. "I guess it's not the end of the world if we don't get the crown ruby for Maryrose."

Wait, what?

"What are you talking about?" I ask him. "Of course it is."

"I'm just saying it's not the worst thing if she doesn't get stronger."

"Yes it is! Jonah! What's going on with you? Why does it seem like you don't want to help Maryrose?"

He frowns and kicks at a pebble.

"I do," he says. "But . . . once Maryrose gets her fairy powers back, she'll leave — and take Prince with her."

Oh. So that's why Jonah is being weird.

"No, she won't," I say. "Prince is *our* dog."

"But he wanted to stay with Maryrose," Jonah says with a pout. "He really likes her. Plus, they're both from the fairy tale world. Maybe he wants to be her dog."

I stop walking and stare at Jonah. Prince wouldn't choose Maryrose over us. Would he? No. I shake my head. "Prince is just watching over Maryrose while she's weak," I assure him.

"I don't know," he says, kicking at another pebble. "I guess we'll see."

Okay, I admit I'm not one hundred percent sure of anything. But I really don't think Prince will leave with Maryrose. We don't even know where she'll go. Or if she'll stop taking us into stories.

"Really, don't worry," I tell Jonah, trying to sound confident.

We walk along quietly.

"If you could be named any number, what would you pick?" Jonah asks me, breaking the silence.

"I wouldn't want to be named a number," I say.

"You can call me Seven And Three Quarters," he says. "'Cause that's how old I am."

"But then your name would change every few months."

"It could change every minute!"

"Oh, Seven And Nine Months And Six Days And Seven Minutes — "

"Now Eight Minutes — "

"Mom and Dad would mess it up all the time."

"And I'd forget to answer."

"Classroom attendance would be tough."

He laughs. Then he stops.

"Abby, look!" Jonah says, pointing. "The pebbly path that Terry was talking about!"

I peer up ahead. He's right. There's a path covered in white pebbles.

We follow it.

Wait. I hear something. Music?

"Jonah, do you hear that?" I ask.

"I think someone is humming," he says.

I strain to listen. He's right. Someone is definitely humming.

"I guess we follow the hum," I say.

The humming is getting louder. We stop behind a tree, then poke our heads out to see.

A woman is collecting flowers from the ground. She's

putting them in a basket and humming to herself. Nearby is a yellow hut.

She has to be Minerta, right?

"You might as well show yourselves," she says, adding some pebbles to her basket. "I know you're there."

Oops. We step forward. Minerta is very, very, very old. Way older than my nana even. She has wrinkled skin, and her glowing white hair is cut into a bob that ends at her chin. She has sharp bangs just above her eyebrows. She's wearing a shiny purple dress with white flowers on it and a fringe on the bottom that shakes when she moves.

"How did you know we were behind that tree?" Jonah asks.

"Fairies have their ways," she says with a chuckle. "And we don't reveal our secrets."

"Are you Minerta?" I ask.

"I am. Who's asking?"

"Maryrose sent us," I say. "She said you might be able to help."

Minerta stops plucking flowers and looks at me. "Maryrose? The fairy who was cursed and trapped in that mirror?"

"The one and only," Jonah says.

"Oh, that poor dear," Minerta says, shaking her head. "Such a terrible situation. I wish I could have helped her, but my powers have never been too strong to start with. Not like Maryrose's."

"That's the thing," I say. "She's now really weak. She's free from the mirror, but she keeps fading in and out. I think she's getting weaker."

"Ooh," Minerta says. "That's not good. That means she barely has any magic left, you know."

Oh, no!

"Maryrose sent us to Douze to find the crown ruby," I say quickly. "She said it contains healing properties for fairies."

"Well, then you must get it for her," Minerta says.

"We will," I say. "But we need the invisibility cloak for our plan to work. Maryrose said if we need help, we should find you. So here we are. Will you help us? Pretty please?"

"Pretty please with a cherry on top?" Jonah asks. "If you like cherries, that is."

"The invisibility cloak?" Minerta repeats.

"Yes. Can you give it to us?"

"I do have just the one . . ."

"Perfect! Can we have it? To help Maryrose?"

"Well . . ." Minerta hesitates. "I guess I could make another one . . . Okay. Fairies help fairies." Minerta snaps her fingers and extends her hand out like she's holding something. "Here you go."

"Um . . . I don't see anything," I say.

"It's invisible! Here, take it."

"Is this an *Emperor's New Clothes* situation?" Jonah asks.

I reach over and try to take what's in her hand. I don't expect to feel anything . . . but I do. Oh!

"I feel it!" It's cool, and kind of scratchy. I pull the invisible material over my head. I can't tell how big it is exactly. "Does it work?" I ask.

"Yes!" Jonah exclaims. "I can't see you!"

"Really?" I look at my arms. I can see them. But Jonah can't?

"Really," Jonah says. "I can only hear you. You totally disappeared. So awesome."

It works! Hurrah! "Thank you so much," I tell Minerta, taking off the cloak.

"You're welcome," Minerta says, heading toward her yellow hut. "I wish Maryrose the best of luck. I'll be thinking about her."

"Let me try, let me try!" Jonah says, grabbing for the cloak.

Jonah tries on the cloak — and he's invisible! Ha! Then I try it on again and then, finally, we start the long walk back to the castle. By the time we get to the edge of the woods and see the castle grounds, the sun has gone down and it's completely dark.

We run over to the castle. I open the side door and look inside. It's late, so the coast should be clear.

But the coast is *not* clear. Two maids are walking down the hall, holding baskets of laundry.

I pull my head out super fast.

"What's wrong?" Jonah whispers.

"The maids will see us," I explain.

"Um, no they won't," Jonah says with a grin. And he slips under the invisibility cloak.

"Oh, right! Smart, Jonah!"

"Thanks."

I duck in beside him and hold the cloak securely over us. It's still scratchy. But at least that way we know it's there.

Then, hidden under the cloak, Jonah and I step into the castle.

Oh, no. Two more maids turn the corner. They're coming right toward us!

I hold my breath. Jonah holds his breath.

The maids go right past us.

We're invisible! Yay, the cloak really works!

Jonah pumps his fist. "It's like we're superheroes!" he whispers.

"Shhh," I tell him. "The cloak makes us invisible, not silent."

Invisible, we hurry down the hall. Now all we have to do is give the cloak to Prince Gene so he can follow the princesses.

Prince Gene is our only shot. We don't have time to wait for someone else to come along and figure out where the princesses go. Maryrose's fate hinges on *this* prince.

We reach the hallway outside the princesses' room and see Prince Gene sitting at his usual table with his back to us.

"Prince Gene," I whisper. "We did it! We got your invisibility cloak!"

He doesn't answer.

"It's us!" I whisper again.

He still doesn't answer.

"Prince Gene?"

We step around the table and see . . . the prince's eyes are closed. And he's snoring.

He is fast asleep. Again.

"Nooooo!" I cry, shaking his shoulder. "Wake up! You have to wake up!"

He just snores louder.

"Seriously?" Jonah mutters.

I look at the silver cup on the table. It's empty.

"Oh, no," I say. "It seems like he drank whatever was in the cup."

"But we told him not to!" Jonah says.

"And it was his *only* job! How could he have messed that up?"

"Now what?" Jonah asks.

"We have to stay under the invisibility cloak," I say. "And follow the princesses ourselves."

chapter seven

Mystery Solved

At midnight, we watch the princesses open their trap-door. We wait until the last princess disappears beneath the door, closing it behind her. Then, under the invisibility cloak, Jonah and I tiptoe into the bedroom.

Holding the cloak over us with one hand, I carefully open the trapdoor, and we wiggle through it. It's not easy. We keep bumping into each other as we make our way down a winding flight of steep steps. I can see the princesses below us descending the steps as well.

"Don't trip!" I whisper to Jonah.

Princess Twelve glances up at the noise. We freeze. Thankfully, she keeps going.

The stairs end in a small room with no windows. The princesses are gathered together, all looking glamorous in their colorful outfits and brand-new black patent-leather shoes. There are no prim pink uniforms or tight buns. The sisters all wear their hair in different styles — loose and flowing, high ponytails, braids. It's fun to see them showing off their personalities through their fashion.

I really like what Princess Eleven is wearing. It's a flowy red tunic over striped leggings. I wish I had something like that to wear to the school dance on Saturday night.

IF I was going, that is. I'm probably not.

Jonah and I stay silent under our cloak, and it works — no one even glances in our direction.

I watch Princess One turn to face a stone wall. She pushes a button that's so small and faded you can barely see it.

A door slides open.

Aha! A secret exit.

The princesses hurry out, and Jonah and I quickly follow them into the night.

Outside, Princess One presses another button, also very hard to see, on the side of the door. The secret door slides back shut.

So sneaky.

Without making a sound, the princesses run past a huge stand of trees so tall they reach the dark sky. Behind the trees is a sparkling river. Six empty boats are lined up at the dock, waiting.

We watch One and Two climb into the first boat. Three and Four climb into the second, and so on. Finally, Eleven and Twelve climb into the last boat. Each princess picks up an oar. Hmm, if I were in charge of the distribution, I would have put Twelve with One, to even it out in terms of strength. But anyway.

"Where should we go?" Jonah whispers.

"With the youngest ones?" I say. "Less likely to be suspicious."

We carefully get into the boat with Eleven and Twelve. It kind of wobbles.

Eleven makes a face at Twelve. "Stop making the boat rock!" she says.

"I'm not," Twelve insists.

Eleven rolls her eyes.

Sorry! I say in my head.

Eleven and Twelve don't look much alike. Eleven has brown curly hair that's similar to mine, pale skin, and blue eyes. Twelve has straight black hair, brown skin, and brown eyes, and she's wearing a bright blue jumpsuit.

I remember from breakfast this morning that Twelve is the one who likes tap dancing.

I turn to Jonah and hold a finger to my lips. Jonah nods, understanding.

Eleven and Twelve row the boat together across the water. A breeze off the river makes the invisibility cloak flutter, but I keep it in place with my hands.

"Thanks for practicing with me today, Twyla," Eleven says as they row.

Twyla? Oh! That must be Twelve's name for herself, the way Three called herself Terry when we met her.

Was Twyla helping her sister practice tap dancing?

"No problem, Ellie," Twyla says.

Eleven = Ellie. Got it.

"I'm sorry I can't give you any real competition," Twyla adds. "You are the queen of chess!"

Chess? Oh! I bet it was Ellie's chessboard I noticed under the bed yesterday.

"Thanks. I really enjoy it," Ellie tells her sister as she rows. "I can't wait for the competition."

"When is it again?"

"The day after tomorrow. At four o'clock in the afternoon."

Twyla gasps. "Ellie! No!"

"What?" Ellie asks.

"The chess tournament is the exact same day and time as our ballet recital!"

Ellie's face falls. She looks like she might cry.

"I was hoping that I could sneak out to the tournament and no one would notice," she says. "But that will be hard to do when I'm supposed to be onstage."

"All of Father's fancy friends will be watching, too," Twyla says.

"I hate that he won't let me play chess!" Ellie frowns and stares out at the dark river. Poor Ellie.

"So unfair," Jonah whispers to me.

Ellie turns to Twyla. "Did you hear something?" she asks.

"No," Twyla says. "That must have been from another boat. Voices carry on the water."

Whew. That was close.

"Ooh, we're here!" Princess Eight in the next boat calls out.

"Yay!" Twyla says, and Ellie smiles, perking up.

The boats approach a stone archway. One by one, the boats ahead of us go through the arch and . . .

Disappear.

"Whoa," Jonah whispers.

I'm too shocked to shush him. Where did the boats go?

I guess we're about to find out.

Twyla and Ellie row right through the archway and then pull in their oars. Now we're on a platform. Suddenly, the platform lowers and the boat is pulled into a tunnel.

A secret tunnel! I look at Jonah, and he's grinning.

So cool, he mouths to me. I nod. It really is.

The tunnel shoots sideways, carrying the boat forward like a roller coaster. Whee! I hang on to Jonah so he won't slip out from under the cloak. Finally, the boat arrives at the mouth of the tunnel and emerges onto a riverbank. Looming above the riverbank is a large stone building. Amazingness! A secret underground moat and castle!

The other boats are pulling up to the dock. A gentleman in a fancy uniform helps each princess from the boat onto the dock, and the princesses head through a stone doorway that leads into the building. I can hear music and laughing inside.

Jonah and I hold the invisibility cloak tight over us, and we stand up, making the boat wobble.

Hmm. It's not like the man in uniform can help us onto the dock, since he can't see us.

"Don't trip on the bottom of the cloak," I warn Jonah.

"I won't," he says. "I hope I won't."

I grimace and stare into the choppy water. I would not want to fall overboard into that. I'm pretty sure I see something green and brown slithering just under the surface. Crocodiles? Why are there always crocodiles in fairy tales?

We oh-so-carefully manage to get ourselves off the boat without falling in the water.

Then we follow Twyla and Ellie through the doorway into the secret castle.

chapter eight

Shoe Scuffing

We step inside a huge room with stone walls and a stone floor. But it's not like any fairy tale room we've seen before. There are disco balls flashing, music blasting from a DJ stand, and a table with a punch bowl, silver goblets, and snacks. There's also an enormous dance floor, and a ton of people of all ages are dancing. Everyone is wearing colorful outfits. It's a big party! Like my cousin's bar mitzvah but bigger, and underground.

It's amazing. And kind of intimidating.

Jonah and I stand in a corner out of the way so no one bumps into us. I keep the invisibility cloak tight around us.

I glance up at the stone wall. A huge tapestry is hung that reads:

DRP — DANCE RESISTANCE PARTY

KINGDOM OF DOUZE DANCERS UNITE!

TAP, JAZZ, HIP-HOP, MODERN, FREESTYLE,

FUNKY CHICKEN . . . ALL DANCE IS WELCOME HERE!

Oh, oh, oh! "Jonah! I get what this is!"

"Is it a bar mitzvah?" he responds.

"No. We're at a resistance party for dance!"

"A what?" he asks, scrunching up his face.

I think about how to explain it. "King LaPear outlawed all dance except ballet, right? So a group of people who want to do other kinds of dancing must have started the resistance. They're *resisting* the law! And so they created a secret dance hall. Everyone can dance however they want here."

"So here I can do the robot dance?" Jonah asks.

"Um, I guess."

Jonah starts to move his arms like a robot under the cloak. He almost punches me in the nose.

"Oops, sorry," he says.

Maybe being bad at dancing is a trait we share.

Anyway, I need to focus on the princesses. I briefly lost

sight of them when Jonah and I walked inside, but now I spot all twelve of them in the center of the dance floor. They're all laughing and dancing, and acting very differently from how they behaved — stiff and formal — at the breakfast table with their father this morning.

I watch Terry, the princess we met, the one who likes gymnastics and has a secret crush. Her dance style is almost acrobatic — lots of jumps and even a cartwheel. Princess One is doing an old-fashioned-looking dance that I think is called the Charleston. She's wearing a sleeveless dress with black fringes swinging from the hem. Princess Seven, wearing a purple dress embroidered with little stars, is dancing with another girl in the crowd; I think they're doing a tango.

Some people are slow dancing, some are dancing super fast, some are break dancing, and a bunch of girls are tap dancing, including Twyla. She has a huge smile on her face.

Princess Four starts a conga line, and all twelve princesses join in, holding on to the hips of the person in front of them and kicking their legs out to the side. No wonder their shoes get so worn down. But I have to admit it looks like they're having a blast. I think about my school dance again, but then I push the thought away.

The DJ plays all different kinds of music — rock, pop,

hip-hop, country, Broadway show tunes. The next song that comes on is one of my favorites. I start tapping my foot to the music.

"You should go dance!" Jonah says. "Without the cloak, I mean. No one will know that you don't belong. There are a ton of people here."

I stop tapping my foot. "No! No way." I shake my head. Doesn't Jonah remember THE INCIDENT?

Before I can remind him, he lets out a yawn. Then another.

It is definitely past his bedtime. "Why don't you go rest under the refreshment table?" I say, pointing. The table has a long gold tablecloth that reaches the floor, so he'll be hidden and safe there. "I'll keep the cloak and go look for the proof we need."

Jonah yawns again. "Good plan. But let's have a snack first."

It's true that we haven't eaten anything since our donuts this morning. We hurry over to the table and sneak some punch and chips under the cloak. Then we crawl under the table and take off the cloak. Jonah lies down on his belly. In two seconds, he's out cold. How he can sleep when the music is so loud is beyond me.

I pull the cloak over me and slip out from under the table. I gaze around the crowded room, wondering what I could take as proof.

Princess Four is now singing at the top of her lungs to the song playing. Ellie and Twyla are dancing together, bumping hips and giggling.

Terry is looking around the room with a hopeful expression. I wonder if she's hoping her secret crush will show up here.

Suddenly, the music stops. I hear groans. A few people call out, "It can't be three o'clock already!"

"Sorry, folks," the DJ announces from his booth. "It is three A.M. But we'll see you again tomorrow night at the DRP — Dance Resistance Party!"

I watch as the crowd begins to disperse. The princesses start saying good-bye to their friends. There are hugs and cries of "See you tomorrow!" and then the princesses head for the stone doorway that leads to the boats.

It's time to go — but I don't have the proof yet!

I need something that will show the king where the princesses were.

I look all around. What can I take? I need something easy to carry.

My gaze stops on the refreshment table. The silver goblets! They each have the letters DRP stamped on them.

Yes! Perfect!

I grab one goblet and hurry back under the table. Jonah is still sleeping!

I shake him awake. He sits up and rubs his eyes.

"That was an awesome nap," he says.

"Time to head back. Look," I say, holding out the goblet. "I have the proof we need. Our plan is working!"

Jonah bites his lip. "Oh. I guess that's good."

"Right," I say. I can tell he's still worried that Prince will want to leave with Maryrose when she regains her powers. But we don't have time to discuss that now! The boats are about to leave. If they do, we'll be stranded here.

With the cloak secure around us, Jonah and I rush out of the dance hall. The princesses' boats are just starting to pull out. Oh, no! Jonah and I hurry toward Ellie and Twyla's boat.

It's not easy getting into a boat while holding an invisibility cloak over you and carrying a goblet.

As we step inside, the boat wobbles.

"Twyla!" Ellie snaps. "Careful!"

"It wasn't me!" Twyla insists.

I grab the edge of the boat to steady myself.

And the silver goblet falls out of my hand and right into the water.

Nooo!

What do I do, what do I do?

Jonah crouches like he's about to jump in the water to get the goblet, but I grab his hoodie and hold him back. Did he not see the crocodiles?

And Twyla and Ellie are already rowing the boat. We're on our way back to the castle.

Without the proof!

I watch the goblet float farther and farther from us.

Crumbs. Double crumbs. Triple crumbs!

I take a deep breath and look at my watch. Okay. It's 3:00 A.M. here, which means it's a little after 2:30 A.M. at home. We still have another night. The prince will just have to come back tomorrow and get the proof.

He can do it. *We* can do it. I know we can.

As they row, Ellie and Twyla talk about how much fun they had at the dance. I try to listen, but it's hard to focus. I'm so annoyed at myself for dropping the goblet. Why was I so clumsy? It was almost as bad as THE INCIDENT. Thank goodness I didn't try to dance tonight. I could have accidentally burned down the whole place or something.

The boats arrive back at the riverbank, and the princesses get out. Under our cloak, Jonah and I watch as the princesses run past the row of trees and into the castle. Then Jonah and I hurry over to where the secret entrance is.

"I want to push the button!" Jonah says.

Of course he does.

"Go ahead," I say.

He grins, but then his smile fades. He stares at the outside of the castle. "Uh, Abby, where's the button?"

I look all over. I don't see it, either. Oh, no.

What happens if we can't find it? We'll be stuck outside all night!

I step really close, my nose practically touching the stone. My nose bumps into something.

"There!" I say. Now I see it. A tiny button the same color as the stones.

Jonah pushes it, and the door slides open. Once we're inside, he finds the button to close the door, and we rush up the steps to the trapdoor. Princesses One and Two are at the top of the steps. As they go up into the bedroom, we dart in, too, right before One closes the trapdoor.

Whew, we made it.

Like last night, the princesses take off their scuffed, worn-down shoes as they talk and laugh about the party.

I notice Princesses One and Two leaving the bedroom. I nudge Jonah, and we follow them to see what they're up to.

"Whose shoe is that?" Princess Two asks, glancing back at us.

I freeze and look down. Jonah's foot isn't under the cloak. It's out in the open! And they can see it! I poke him and point to his sneaker.

Oops, he mouths, and pulls his foot back under.

Two people sharing one invisibility cloak is not ideal.

Princess Two blinks. "I must be seeing things."

Careful not to let our feet show, Jonah and I follow Princesses One and Two into the hallway. They stop and look down at the sleeping prince. He's snoring loudly, his face smushed against the table. Princesses One and Two smile and high-five each other.

Terry comes into the hallway and stares at Prince Gene. She sighs and shakes her head, then goes back into the bedroom with her sisters.

I sigh, too. Prince Gene has no idea how important he

is! Tomorrow night, he'll stay awake, follow the princesses, take a goblet for proof, NOT drop it in the moat, and then everything will fall into place. He'll tell the king what he saw, get the crown, and give us the ruby.

The plan has to work. Maryrose's fairy powers depend on it.

chapter nine

Invisible

Jonah and I sneak through the castle under our invisibility cloak, looking for a good empty bedroom to sleep in. We find a pale blue room with two twin beds and decide to camp out there for the night. Jonah plops onto one bed and sneezes — the bed frames are kind of dusty. They clearly haven't been used in a while. At least I can lock the door, so we don't have to sleep under the cloak.

Even though Jonah had his nap at the Dance Resistance Party, he falls asleep immediately. I climb into the other bed, not sure I'll be able to sleep since I'm so worried about Maryrose and the plan. But I must be exhausted, since I fall asleep right away, too.

The next morning, the loud chime we heard yesterday wakes us up. Sunlight is streaming through the arched windows. That chime must be what calls the princesses to breakfast. Through our locked door, I hear the twelve sisters making their way to the dining room.

"Let's go," I whisper to Jonah.

We get up, huddle under the cloak, and slip out of the bedroom. Invisible, we enter the dining room and watch a replay of yesterday's breakfast: The princesses sit primly at the table in their pink uniforms, tight buns, and scuffed shoes; the king says good morning by calling the princesses numbers one through twelve; the maids serve a delicious-looking breakfast (my stomach growls under the cloak — oops); the king asks the princesses what they did last night to scuff their shoes and they don't answer; Prince Gene is called in, and he admits he doesn't know what the princesses did. The king tells him he has ONE more chance — his LAST chance — to prove himself (yikes), and then breakfast is over.

Jonah and I wait until the king, the maids, and the princesses have left the room. Only Prince Gene remains, hanging out by the cart of breakfast leftovers. He looks confused and miserable. It's time to talk to him.

Jonah and I take off our cloak.

"Ahhh!" Prince Gene yelps. "You've got to stop jumping out at people like that!"

"Sorry," I say. I hold up the cloak. "Remember the invisibility cloak we told you about? This is it. We used it last night to follow the princesses. Because someone who was *supposed* to do that was fast asleep."

His cheeks turn bright red, and he bites his lip. "Sorry. I don't know what happened. I asked for strong coffee and that's what I drank. Coffee!"

"Well, obviously the coffee didn't work," Jonah says with a frown.

"They must have put a sleeping potion in the coffee," I say. "You really should not drink anything they give you."

"Anyhoo," the prince says, his face brightening. "No need to dwell on that! Because you two followed the princesses. So you got the proof of where they go? We good?"

Now it's my turn to bite my lip.

"Uh, I *did* get proof," I say sheepishly. "But I accidentally dropped it in the moat. There are snapping crocodiles in there."

"Lots of them," Jonah confirms.

"Uh-oh," the prince says.

Yeah. "Look, Prince Gene," I say. "Tonight is it. Our last chance."

He swallows. "I know."

"If you want to survive," I say. "If you want to be heir to the kingdom and live happily ever after, do not drink anything given to you tonight. Not a thing."

"Not a drop," Jonah adds. "Although I guess Abby and I could follow the princesses again if we have to."

"No!" The prince lifts his chin. "I can do it. I know I can!" He glances at my hand. "Are you holding the cloak right now? Can I try it on?"

"Sure," I say, and hold it out to him.

He carefully steps into it. And then he disappears.

"Can you see me?" Prince Gene asks.

"Nope," Jonah tells him.

"I can see *you*," the prince says, sounding worried.

"That's because we're not invisible," I point out.

"Oh, right," Prince Gene says. "Excellent. Why is it so scratchy?"

"It just is," I say.

"Hmm," we hear the invisible prince say, "maybe I should try to wash it."

Uh-oh. Knowing Prince Gene, he'd try that and somehow mess with the cloak's magic. Or lose the cloak entirely!

"No," Jonah jumps in, clearly thinking the same thing. "You should give the cloak back to us now. You don't need it until tonight."

"Yes, that's probably for the best," I add firmly.

"Okay," the prince says with a shrug.

He reappears and hands the cloak to me just as we hear footsteps approaching the dining room. Jonah and I immediately slip the cloak back over us.

Terry — also known as Three — comes into the room, and she smiles when she sees Prince Gene.

"Oh, hi," she says, her cheeks turning pink. "I just came to get another donut."

"They are very good," the prince says, helping himself to one, too.

"Are you nervous about tonight?" Terry asks him. "I'm sure you'll succeed."

The prince puffs out his chest. "I'll get some proof tonight, for sure! The coffee seemed to have the wrong effect last night. It was supposed to keep me awake."

Terry sighs sadly.

"I have tonight to make up for it," he says. "And I will! I'm a prince, for royal's sake!"

Terry looks around. Then back at the prince.

I have the feeling she wants to tell him the truth. Or help him in some way.

But she's one of the twelve dancing princesses. She won't say anything that will get her sisters — and herself — in trouble. Will she?

"Good luck," she finally says, and darts out of the dining room.

"Aww, she feels bad for him," I whisper to Jonah. "Oh wait," I say, realizing something, "maybe he's her crush!"

Oh, oh! If Terry likes the prince, maybe he can marry her instead of choosing the oldest princess, who obviously doesn't like the prince. Then everyone wins!

"Can we have some donuts?" Jonah whispers back. "I'm so hungry."

"You two can stop being invisible now," the prince tells us. "It's just me here."

I pull off the cloak. I guess it would have been fine for Terry to see us, since she thinks we're cooks at the castle. But it's so convenient to just use the cloak.

"I'm going outside to practice my eye exercises again," the prince tells us.

"Okay," I say, picking up a donut. "We'll see you this evening in front of the princesses' bedroom. And, Prince Gene? Isn't Terry so great?"

"She does seem very nice," he says before leaving the dining room.

Oh, I hope he chooses her.

"I have an idea," Jonah says through a mouthful of donut. "Since we have the cloak all day, why don't we have some fun? We can explore the castle this way!"

"Hmm," I say. "Okay. But we need to be careful."

"Wahoo!" Jonah says. "Invisible vacation day, here we come!"

We explore the whole castle, and we find a library, a gym, the classrooms where the girls have their school lessons, and even the fancy auditorium where they will have their ballet recital. Terry was right; they never have to leave the castle. But I can see how the princesses might feel a bit trapped. Maybe that's why they are so determined to sneak out every night.

Under our cloak, though, Jonah and I are free to do what we please. We sneak food from the kitchen. We read books in the library. In the gym, I ride on the stationary bike and Jonah tries out the rowing machine. He's really good at it! No wonder the princesses are so good at rowing — they can practice whenever!

Before we know it, it's nighttime, and we have to go meet Prince Gene outside the princesses' bedroom.

Prince Gene is sitting in his usual chair when we arrive under our cloak. Princess One is standing in front of Gene, holding a tray.

"Compliments of the palace kitchen," she tells him, setting it down on his table.

"Ooh, thank you," Prince Gene says, and I see Princess One smile and slip a tiny flask into her pocket. OMG. Did she pour some sort of sleeping potion into something on the tray? She must have.

"Good night, Prince," Princess One says, still with that mischievous smile, and she heads back into her bedroom to join her sisters.

Jonah and I run up behind Prince Gene.

"It's us," I whisper to the prince. "Remember, do not drink ANYTHING!"

"Got it," he says. "No drinking!"

"Good," Jonah says.

"But I am going to try this mint chocolate chip ice cream, because it's my favorite flavor." I hear a spoon clink against the side of a bowl.

What?

"Noooooo," I tell him.

"But it's delicious!" the prince says, his mouth full of ice cream.

I reach my hand out from under the cloak to try and stop him.

But it's too late. The prince's eyes close, and he slumps forward. The spoon drops out of his hand and onto the floor with a little clang.

I shake my head.

He's out cold. And snoring.

"Was there a sleeping potion in the ice cream?" Jonah whispers.

"Yup," I say.

Jonah shrugs. "I probably would have fallen for that, too. Especially if they put a sleeping potion in ketchup."

Princess One peeks out of the bedroom to see the snoring prince. "He's asleep!" she calls triumphantly to her sisters.

Jonah and I hurry to the bedroom doorway. We watch as all the princesses leap out of their beds, wearing their pink pajamas, and rush into their huge closet to change.

"I guess we're going to the dance party again?" Jonah whispers to me.

"I guess so," I say.

Five minutes later, the princesses emerge from the closet in their fun, funky outfits.

Twyla grabs her new black shoes and sits on her bed. She reaches into her bedside table and pulls something out. I watch her stick whatever it is on the bottoms of her shoes. Then she stands up and does a little tap dance. Stick-on taps! Fun! How awesome would those be on sneakers?

Princess One lifts open the trapdoor. "Let's go!" she calls.

"The moment the last princess is down the hatch," I whisper to Jonah, "we run after them."

"Got it," he says.

All twelve princesses disappear through the trapdoor. As soon as Twyla goes down, Jonah and I rush over before the trapdoor closes, and we race down the stairs. We dash out the secret exit right before Princess One closes it. The princesses run to the riverbank, and Jonah and I are right behind them.

Lined up are the same six rowboats. The princesses all get in, two to a boat. Once again, Jonah and I get into the boat with Ellie and Twyla.

"Do you think there's any way I can go to the chess tournament tomorrow?" Ellie asks as they row along the water.

"I doubt it," Twyla says. "How could you possibly miss the ballet recital?"

"I don't know," Ellie says sadly. "Argh, why is Father so strict?"

Poor Ellie. I wish there was some way I could help her.

Focus, Abby, I tell myself. First Jonah and I have to get the proof from the party tonight and NOT drop it in the moat.

Just like last night, our boat goes under the awesome secret tunnel, and we emerge onto the hidden riverbank with the stone castle. The princesses disembark and hurry inside. Jonah and I, carefully keeping the cloak secure around us, get off the boat and follow them.

We're back!

The dance hall looks just as amazing as it did last night, with the DRP banner and the DJ. But since I've been here before, it feels less intimidating, too.

The disco ball sends rays of glitter over all the dancers, and I can't help but do a little twirl. It's not like anyone can see me, anyway.

All the princesses start dancing, some with girls, some with boys. I see Terry dancing with Four and Five. She's doing flips, and a small crowd forms around her to cheer and clap. I wish I had the guts to do what she's doing!

Speaking of guts, my stomach is growling. I motion to Jonah, and we slide over to the refreshment table and nab some chocolate chunk cookies.

"Okay," I say as we chew our cookies under the cloak. "I'm going to take another goblet as proof."

Jonah smiles. "Maybe *I* should hold on to it this time."

I stick out my tongue. But honestly, maybe he should.

Because if we don't return with proof, it's off with the prince's head.

Which is bad enough on its own. But it also means we won't get the crown ruby for poor Maryrose. What will happen to her then? Will she just get weaker and weaker? What if she disappears entirely?

Failure is not an option!

On the refreshments table, there are plenty of silver goblets with DRP stamped on them. I quickly grab one and stuff it under the cloak. Suddenly, I feel the scratchy cloak rub against my head, like it's falling.

Oh, no.

The scratchiness is gone. I feel the warm air of the room on my hands and face. Someone must have stepped on the back of the cloak, and now it's slipped off me.

I'm exposed, for everyone to see.

chapter ten

Nicknames

abby!" I hear.

"Jonah?" I turn around to look for my brother, but he's still invisible under the cloak.

"What happened?" he whispers.

"I don't know! I slipped out. Cover me!"

Before Jonah can fling the cloak over me, someone puts their hand on my shoulder.

"You!" a voice says.

I freeze. And carefully turn around. It's Terry.

She can see me. I mean, of course she can see me. I'm no longer invisible!

"Um, hi," I say. Is she going to have me thrown out? For

crashing an underground party *and* stealing a goblet? I'm obviously not dressed up for the party — I'm wearing my jeans and hoodie.

She smiles. "So great to see you here, Chef! I'm glad the royal staff gets to join the resistance and have fun."

I'm totally confused for a second. Then I remember. She thinks I'm a cook in the palace.

"Yeah, it's great," I echo.

"Come dance with me and my sisters!" she says, taking my arm.

"Oh . . . no, thanks," I say, squirming away. "I, um, don't dance."

Terry frowns, looking the tiniest bit suspicious. "If you don't dance, why are you at the Dance Resistance Party?"

Crumbs. That's a very good point. And I can't exactly say, *Well, I'm here to spy on you and your sisters so I can get the crown ruby for my fairy friend back home,* can I?

"Ha ha, just kidding," I say, trying to think of an excuse not to dance. "I need to, um, finish my drink."

I pretend to drink from my empty goblet. Since Terry is watching me, I have no choice but to "finish" my pretend drink and put the goblet on the table. Hopefully, Jonah — wherever he is — will pick it up.

"Great! Now come dance!" Terry says, and before I can protest, she drags me onto the dance floor.

Terry starts to dance. I stand still, feeling super awkward as she bumps my hip with hers and giggles. People are dancing all around us. They are looking at me with curiosity. I take a deep breath. Okay. If I'm going to fit in here and seem like a regular Douze citizen who likes to dance, I have to actually . . . dance.

I move one foot, then another. So far, so good. I haven't knocked anyone over. And no one is mocking me.

Terry high-fives me, which makes me feel better, too.

Just then, two of her sisters dance over to us.

"I love your outfit," Princess Four says to me as she shimmies her shoulders. "So unique!"

I laugh. "Thanks," I say. I guess, here, jeans and a hoodie are unique. "I love yours, too." She's wearing a green jumpsuit and a tiny, sparkly green hat with a feather sticking out.

"I'm Fanny," she tells me. "And this is my twin sister, Franny!" she adds, pointing at Princess Five.

They're several years older than me, with blue eyes, pale skin, and long blond hair.

Franny smiles and starts jumping up and down and

moving her arms every which way. The song playing is a poppy folk song. I clap my hands to the beat.

"As you can see," Franny shouts over the music, "I'm a terrible dancer. But I don't care. I love to dance anyway!"

"You're not bad, Fran," Fanny says. "What is 'bad' anyway? Who gets to decide what's good dancing and what's bad dancing? Dancing is about enjoying the music. And anyway, no one is watching you." She winks. "Everyone is having too much fun to notice that you keep elbowing me in the ribs by accident."

Franny laughs. "Sorry!" She twirls around — and elbows her twin right in the ribs. "Oops! Sorry again!"

They both giggle and raise their arms in the air, shaking their hips and kicking out their legs.

I watch them, thinking about what Fanny said. Maybe she's right. Maybe there's no such thing as "good" or "bad" dancing. Maybe it's okay to be clumsy, even if everyone sees you messing up. Maybe it's all about just having fun.

I move my feet some more, and suddenly, I'm doing it. I'm dancing! I clap and kick my legs, and then I jump up and down.

"Nice!" Terry tells me approvingly.

I smile, feeling flushed. "Thanks!" I say.

When the song changes to what sounds like a Broadway show tune, Twyla joins us and starts tap dancing. I follow her moves, even though my sneakers don't make a peep.

The funny thing is, I'm not thinking about THE INCIDENT or worrying that people are judging me for being a bad dancer.

Maybe I am a bad dancer. But who cares?

Dancing is fun!

I feel a poke in my left side. I glance around. No one's standing on my left.

"Abby," I hear Jonah whisper. "It's me!"

Oh, right. My invisible brother.

"Having fun?" he asks.

"I am," I say. Hmm. Maybe I should reconsider going to the school dance.

The music stops. A chorus of "Aww, it can't be three A.M.!" comes from the crowd.

"I could dance all night," Twyla says, giving another few taps.

"Back to the boats!" Princess One calls out to her sisters.

Wait! The goblet I left on the table is still there. We can't leave without our proof.

I point to it, and point to it again, hoping my brother sees.

Suddenly, I see one of the silver goblets moving by itself toward the back of the table. Moving. Moving. Moving.

And now it's gone.

Good job, Jonah.

I guess I should be sneaking under the cloak, too. "Jonah!" I call out quietly. "Come get me!"

"Right here," he says.

I'm about to slip under the cloak when Terry, Fanny, and Franny come running over to me in their seriously scuffed shoes.

"We just realized we didn't get to say good-bye!" Terry says.

"And we don't even know your name," Fanny adds.

"It's Abby," I say. "And this is my — " I stop just in time. I'm so used to introducing Jonah that I almost forgot no one can see him. Not even me.

"Do you live near our castle?" Terry asks.

"Um . . . no. I live kind of far away," I say.

Kind of far? So far.

"Why don't you come home with us?" Terry offers. "I mean, you're going to have to come to the castle in the morning to prepare breakfast anyway, so just sleep over."

"Um . . . Sure?"

Why not? At least I can go with them in the boat as myself. And go to a princess slumber party! Maybe I can also talk to the sisters about the prince. Find out if he is Terry's crush. Or if any of the others like him. I would feel much better about marrying one of them off to Prince Gene if they actually like him.

"Thank you so much," I say.

"Sure thing," Terry says.

"Let's go, princesses," Franny says, waving to her other sisters.

"Ooh, Abby," Terry says. "You can be an honorary princess tonight!"

I like the sound of that.

The twelve princesses head toward the door, and I follow. I hear little footsteps behind me.

When no one is looking, I turn around. "Got the proof, right, Jonah?"

Jonah bumps right into me. Ow.

"Yup," he whispers.

"Make sure you get on the same boat as me!" I say. "Twyla and Ellie's."

"I will," Jonah says.

It is so weird to hear him and not see him. I'm used to constantly hearing him and seeing him. Even when I don't want to.

As I join the princesses outside on the dock, Terry introduces me to the rest of her sisters as Abby, a cook in the castle kitchen.

They all tilt their heads at me.

Princess One says, "Really? I've never seen you before."

"I'm pretty new," I say. "My little brother works with me, too."

"Oh," she says. "Well, I'm Oona. The oldest."

Princess Two smiles. "Hi. I'm Tricia!"

"And you know me," Terry says. "Terry. Otherwise known as Three."

"And me," Fanny says.

"And me too!" Franny adds.

A princess who looks just like the queen from the portrait, with brown skin, dark brown eyes, and dark ringlets, waves. "I'm Sima — otherwise known as Six."

"And I'm Senna," Seven says.

The princess with the short pixie haircut does a pirouette. "Eileen," she says. "Eighth born."

I smile. "I love your hair!"

Eileen grins. "Thanks! My dad was not pleased that I cut it, but it was worth it. He forgave me eventually."

The next princess is petite, with long curly black hair. "I'm Nina," she says. "Otherwise known as Nine." I notice that her T-shirt has a picture of the solar system on it.

"Cool shirt," I tell her.

"Thanks. I'm really into astronomy," she says.

"And I'm Tania, tenth born," her sister behind her says.

Ellie steps forward. "I'm Ellie."

"And I'm Twyla. Twelve," Twyla says, "but I'm eleven years old. The youngest but the wisest!"

All the princesses laugh.

I try to remember all their nicknames.

One — Oona
Two — Tricia
Three — Terry
Four — Fanny
Five — Franny
Six — Sima
Seven — Senna
Eight — Eileen

Nine — Nina

Ten — Tania

Eleven — Ellie

Twelve — Twyla

Yes! Got them all!

"Come in our boat," Ellie says.

That was my plan already. I get in the boat with Ellie and Twyla, and sit on one side of the bench to make room for Jonah.

Don't drop the goblet. Don't drop the goblet. Don't drop the goblet.

I feel Jonah's foot on my toe.

"I have the goblet," he whispers to me.

Whew. "Nicely done," I whisper back.

"What did you say?" Twyla asks, leaning forward to look at me.

I think fast. "Um, that I had a nice time tonight."

Ellie and Twyla each take an oar and begin rowing.

"We did, too," Ellie says as she pushes the left oar in the water.

"Do you all love to dance?" I ask Twyla, and she nods.

"Yes, but we all love *different* kinds of dance," she explains. "Only one of us — Eileen — likes ballet. That's the only type of dance our father allows in the kingdom."

Ellie sighs. "Don't remind me of ballet." She glances at me. "Our annoying ballet recital is tomorrow," she explains. "Our father invites all 'the finest' families from Douze and surrounding kingdoms. And that means I have to skip my chess tournament. I love chess more than anything!"

I've never played chess, but I know it's played on what looks like a checkerboard with cool game pieces, like a knight and a castle.

"I really want to take part in the tournament," Ellie continues. "I don't think I would win, but . . ."

"You might," Twyla says. "You're really good."

"Thanks," she says. "I guess I'll never know how I would have done . . ." Tears fill her eyes. Aw. Poor Ellie. I feel awful.

"You should definitely compete in the tournament," I tell Ellie.

"Really?" Ellie asks me, sniffling. "You think so?"

"Yes!" I say. "You have to put yourself out there. Take a risk. Follow your heart. Otherwise, how will you know what you might achieve?" That's what my mom always says. "Plus, you'll have fun. Maybe you can talk to your dad so he'll let you go?"

"He'll never let me go," she says mournfully. "And I can't sneak out because I'll get caught if I'm missing from the ballet performance. Argh. I hate that he's so controlling."

I feel a wave of guilt. Our plan to help the prince and get the crown ruby isn't going to help Ellie's situation. In fact, it will make it worse. We're basically spilling the princesses' secret! If their dad was controlling before, he's only going to be more controlling when he finds out the truth.

But what choice do we have?

I shake my head, feeling guilty the whole way back to the castle.

chapter eleven

Royal Slumber Party

We arrive back at the castle and go up the stairs to the trapdoor in the princesses' bedroom. I pretend to be surprised, like I've never seen this trapdoor before.

"It does come in handy," Twyla tells me as we emerge into the bedroom.

"Wow," I say. "I bet."

I think I hear Jonah snort under his cloak. I would nudge him if I knew exactly where he was.

As the princesses take off their scuffed shoes, I watch Oona hurry into the hallway outside the bedroom. She peers at the snoring prince with a smile, then glances back at her sisters.

"He's still out cold," she says happily.

"Poor Prince Gene," Senna says. "Tonight was his last chance. I feel kind of bad for him."

"Me too," Franny says.

"Well, it wasn't very smart of him to tell us that mint chocolate chip ice cream was his favorite food earlier today," Fanny says. "We knew he'd gobble it up."

"With the sleeping potion mixed in!" Eileen says.

Terry frowns. "I think Prince Gene is very smart."

Smart? Um . . .

Then again, he *didn't* drink anything. Not a drop, just like he promised. But he should have known not to eat anything, too. Mint chocolate chip ice cream or not.

"He's cute, too," she says, and gets a dreamy look on her face.

Oh, yeah. He's her crush all right. And maybe he likes her, too!

Jonah and I will explain the situation to the prince and let him know that we got the proof for him. And that he should choose Terry to marry. And then our plan can go on as it should.

"I'm so excited that we're having a sleepover," Franny says as she and her sisters head into their closet to change. "Yay for Abby the chef!"

I feel another wave of guilt. Not only did I lie to them about who I am, but I'll be getting them all in big trouble tomorrow.

Their secret will be revealed.

No more underground dance hall.

No more fun.

No more funky outfits.

No more tapping for Twyla.

No more chess for Ellie.

I feel something pressing on my foot again. I look down and see nothing. So obviously it's Jonah.

"Ow," I whisper.

"Sorry," he whispers back. "I'm going to sleep in the blue bedroom again, okay?"

Hmm. I don't love being apart from Jonah when we're inside a fairy tale. But I'm glad he has the cloak to keep him safe. "Okay. Be careful."

"Don't worry," he says. "What could go wrong?"

So many things. "You could lose the goblet."

"I won't," he promises. "What else?"

"Someone could sit on you by accident?"

He giggles. "I'll be careful. Bye!"

"Lock the door!" I whisper, but I think he's already gone.

The princesses come out of the closet, all wearing their pajamas. Thankfully, they didn't catch me talking to myself.

"Here's a pair of pj's for you," Ellie says, handing me a set. "I bet we're the same size, so you can wear one of my extras."

"Thank you," I say.

Eileen drags an air mattress from the closet. "Little help here, please?" she calls out.

Her sisters all rush over to help blow up the mattress. When it's ready, they place it beside Twyla and Ellie's bunk bed. Fanny and Franny grab a fluffy pillow and a soft blanket.

For me. How nice are they? So nice.

I wish they'd stop being so nice.

It's making me feel even guiltier.

"Want a sleep mask?" Sima asks, holding out a pink satin mask.

Senna holds out a small gold tube. "And pear-scented beeswax lip balm?"

"And how about a pair of royal-purple fuzzy sleeping socks?" Tania says, handing them to me.

Yes. Yes, I do. I want it all! The royal treatment, the royal everything!

The princesses are all incredibly kind. Really, really kind. Not a Penny among them.

I sigh again. I think of Maryrose, fading in and out, barely able to stay solid. Her powers so weak.

For her sake, I have to do what I'm doing. I *have* to get that crown ruby.

I just wish I could do it without getting anyone in trouble.

"Abby, wake up! Abby!"

I feel someone nudging my shoulder.

I open my eyes. I'm lying on my air mattress. It's still dark in here.

Ellie's head is hanging over the side of her bottom bunk, her curly hair dangling on the rug. "Abby, I have a huge favor to ask you."

A favor? I can do a favor! That will help me feel less guilty! "What favor?"

She glances around. The other princesses are still sleeping.

Ellie looks back at me, lowering her voice.

"I thought about what you said in the boat," she says.

"That I have to put myself out there. Take risks. Because that's how I'll achieve what I want. That it's about having fun and following my heart."

I smile. "I'm really glad I was able to help."

"So I'm going to participate in the chess tournament today!" she announces.

"Yay!" I say.

"But," she adds, "I have a big problem. The tournament is the same time as the ballet recital. Our father expects to see all *twelve* of his princesses in the recital."

That is definitely a problem.

"He'll freak out if one is missing!" she adds. "Which is where the favor — and you — come in."

"Me?" I ask. How could I help? I mean, it's not like she'll ask me to *fill in* for her. I almost snort at the thought. Me, dancing ballet in a recital! After THE INCIDENT?

"Will you fill in for me?" Ellie asks.

Blink, blink.

"You're — you're kidding, right?" I manage to sputter. "Have you *seen* me dance?"

"Actually, I have. Last night. You're . . . not terrible!"

I tilt my head. "Oh. Really?"

"You have your own style! I would teach you the

routine. And really, you just need to watch my sisters and copy them."

"I don't know, Ellie . . ." I begin, my stomach twisting.

It was one thing to dance however I wanted at the DRP last night. But a ballet recital? In front of the entire kingdom? And surrounding kingdoms?!

"You're my only hope, Abby," Ellie adds. "We're almost the same age. We both have curly brown hair. Your skin color is close to mine. We're the same height. You can pass for me."

It's true. We do kind of look alike.

Hmm. I think about what I said to Ellie in the boat. About putting herself out there. Taking a risk. Finding out what she can achieve.

Doesn't the same go for me?

Ahhh. Why did I say all that? Now I have to take my own advice!

But also: I want to help Ellie. I owe her and her sisters that. Since I'm about to ruin the rest of their lives.

"I'll do it," I tell her.

Her entire face lights up and she reaches over to give me a hug. "Hoorah! Thank you so much, Abby! You're awesome."

"Are you sure your father won't be able to tell that I'm not you?" I ask.

"He always sits in the back, so he won't even notice," Ellie says. "He's more interested in the reaction of the audience, anyway. As long as there are twelve dancing princesses, he's set. It's like he barely knows his own daughters." She shrugs, looking sad. The king is the worst.

"But," Ellie adds in a whisper, "it has to be our secret. I don't want my sisters to know. It's not really fair for me to skip out on them. If I do get caught, it's better if they didn't know and didn't help me."

"I totally understand," I say. "It'll be our secret."

She frowns. "I have one other problem," she adds. "I don't know how I'll get to the tournament by myself. I'm not strong enough to work the oars alone. Twyla and I always row together."

Hmm. Oh! Oh! "I know who can help you row across the river."

"Who?" she asks.

"My little brother, Jonah."

She looks puzzled.

"The one who works with me in the kitchen," I remind

her. "He'll help you." I almost say he was good at the rowing machine in the gym, but that would give away too much.

"Your family is the best," Ellie says.

"Thanks," I say. All I can do is *hope* for the best. And that Jonah and I don't mess everything up.

chapter twelve

Ballerina Princess

bright and early in the morning, the loud chime goes off. The princesses get dressed in their pink uniforms and leave their bedroom.

"You didn't have to prepare breakfast?" Twyla asks me.

"Oh, um, not today! I got the morning off!"

"Wanna come eat with us?" she asks.

"No, thanks," I say, standing in the doorway in my pink pajamas. "I'll get something in the kitchen later." I need to find Jonah and wake up Prince Gene.

I watch as the twelve princesses walk past the sleeping prince. They look at him with pity. They think he failed.

They think it's off-with-his-head time. They think he won't be able to tell the king where they go every night.

But he *will* be able to. With *our* proof.

When all the princesses have gone, Prince Gene is still snoring. I walk over to him, wondering if I should tap his shoulder.

Then I see something weird. The empty bowl — the one that had the ice cream in it — is now balancing on the prince's head.

I hear a giggle.

"Jonah, I know that's you," I whisper. He's having a little too much fun with the invisibility cloak.

The bowl moves from the prince's head to the table.

"Sorry!" Jonah calls out with another giggle. "It seemed like a good idea."

Jonah whips off the cloak. His hair is its usual bedhead mess. And he's holding the goblet. Whew.

Prince Gene's eyes open. He sits up and rubs them. "Uh-oh," he says.

"Uh-oh is right!" I snap.

"You ate the ice cream," Jonah tells him. "The princesses put a sleeping potion in it. So we had to follow them again."

Prince Gene blushes. "You told me not to *drink* anything! Not to not *eat* anything!"

He hangs his head.

I sigh. "Prince Gene, do you *promise* to give us the ruby in the crown in exchange for the information and proof you need to tell the king after the recital?"

He nods. "I promise." He sounds sincere.

"And . . . there's one more thing," I say.

"What is it?" Prince Gene asks.

"You'll win the right to marry any princess of your choosing. But you don't want to marry someone who doesn't want to marry you, right?"

"Of course not," he says.

"Good. So instead of forcing a princess to marry you, I think you should ask her on a date first. What do you say? Deal?"

"Deal," he says.

I lean in closer. "Also, FYI . . . . I'm pretty sure Terry would say yes to a date."

Prince Gene smiles. "That's good to know."

Then I finally tell Prince Gene the entire story. The trapdoor. The secret exit. The boats. The underground building. The dance hall. The resistance movement. The *dancing*.

"Wait, really?" Prince Gene says. "A dance party? Why didn't anyone invite me?"

"It's for the citizens of Douze," I explain.

"Yeah," Jonah adds, "because only ballet is allowed in Douze. And people like to do other kinds of dance."

"Well, I like to dance," Prince Gene says. "I think an underground dance hall is fun."

Jonah hands Prince Gene the goblet. "Here's your proof. See the stamp?"

"Groovy," the prince exclaims, reading the words on the cup. "Thank you both. When I get the crown, I will absolutely, positively give you the ruby."

"Great," I say.

"I'm going to freshen up," the prince says. He carefully tucks the goblet into his blazer pocket. He better not lose it.

Prince Gene heads off. A moment later, Ellie appears in the hallway.

"There you are!" she says to me. "I looked for you in the royal kitchen but couldn't find you."

"I have the day off," I say quickly. "This is my brother, Jonah. He's going to row with you to the chess tournament."

"I am?" my brother asks.

"You are," I say.

"Great," Ellie says. "But I have only two hours to teach you the routine for the recital. Then I'm supposed to be in school with my sisters, so you can practice by yourself."

Does she know who she's dealing with? The Girl Who Knocks Over Other Dancers.

Why did I agree to this?

"Abby's going to dance in a recital?" Jonah asks, looking stunned.

Okay, okay. Let's not overdo the reactions here. I narrow my eyes at Jonah.

"She'll be great," Ellie says.

"That I can't promise," I say.

"I'm going to see if I can get some food," Jonah tells me. He holds up his hand, which means he's holding up the invisibility cloak, so I know he'll wear it around the castle.

"Be safe!" I call to him.

"And meet us back here at three thirty this afternoon," Ellie adds. "So we can row to the tournament."

Jonah nods and runs off.

Ellie leads me into the bedroom and over to the big walk-in closet. She grabs some things off a shelf. "Here," she says. "Put these on." She hands me a leotard, a tutu, and a pair of ballet slippers. "It's our costume for the recital."

Ooh! I have to say, it's always fun to put on a costume. I quickly get changed. The leotard and tutu are pale pink with a darker pink sash around the waist. The tutu is very flouncy. It's actually super cute, and it fits me perfectly, since Ellie and I are the same size.

Ellie ties the pink ballet slippers for me.

I stare at myself in the mirror. I'm a ballerina! A ballerina princess! I give a twirl — and land on my bottom. Oops.

Ellie laughs and helps me up. She leads me over to the far side of the bedroom, where there's space to practice.

"Okay, here's the routine," Ellie says. She raises her arms gracefully in the air.

I try to copy her, but my arms shoot up like a rocket.

"Slower," she says patiently. "And curve your arms a bit."

I try again, and this time Ellie smiles.

"Good!"

Really? Okay!

"Now step to the right," she instructs. "Four steps to the side, arms raised and lowered. Arms raised and lowered. It's pretty simple."

It is NOT simple.

I go left when she says right. I step back when she goes forward.

But after two hours of practicing, I think I've learned the routine. Mostly.

"Now for the bun," Ellie says.

"Huh?" I ask.

She grabs a sparkly black scrunchie and puts it on her wrist. Then she gathers my curly hair on top of my head, twists it into a bun, and secures it with the scrunchie.

"Now you really look like a ballerina," she remarks.

I stare at myself in the mirror. She's right.

Ellie high-fives me. "I know you can do it!" she says.

I might look the part. But can I *dance* the part?

It's three thirty in Douze.

The recital is in a half hour. I'm in the princesses' bedroom, saying good-bye to Ellie and Jonah, who are on their way to the chess tournament. Ellie left school a few minutes early, but the rest of the princesses will be back any minute.

"Good luck," I tell Ellie and Jonah as they disappear down the secret hatch.

"You too!" Ellie calls out.

"Yeah!" Jonah tells me, tucking the invisibility cloak under his arm. "Don't fall or anything."

Gee, thanks.

I hear the princesses coming down the hall. I rush over to Ellie's bed and sit down — facing away. Oh, no. Any second they're going to come in and know I'm not their sister.

The princesses hurry inside their bedroom. There's a rush of activity as they change into their costumes and ballet slippers. At least I'm already in my costume.

"Come on, Ellie!" Oona says to me. "Let's do this."

I stand up. I turn around. But keep my head down. Any chance no one will notice I'm not Ellie?

Like, all eleven of them?

Why didn't we think about this part before?

"Hey! That's not Ellie!" Fanny says, taking one look at me.

I guess not.

"It's Abby!" Franny adds.

"The cook?" Terry asks, looking confused.

I sigh. I guess I have to tell them the truth. What choice do I have? "Ellie is competing in the chess tournament," I tell them.

"I knew it!" Twyla cries.

I nod. "She didn't tell you because she didn't want you all to get in trouble. But you won't. Because I'm going to fill in for her at the recital. I practiced the routine all day. She taught me everything."

"Um . . . okay," Oona says. "I guess Father's expecting twelve dancing princesses, and you make twelve. Just don't mess up."

No kidding.

We leave the bedroom and walk down the hall to the royal auditorium. There are rows of high-backed red velvet seats and a stage with gold satin curtains. Every seat is full. The king, in his royal robes and crown, is sitting in the back row.

I expect him to leap up and point at me and bellow: *You're not Eleven!*

But he doesn't.

I keep my head down and follow the princesses backstage. We line up in birth order. I'm at the end, right before Twyla. Where Ellie would be.

The curtains part. My hands are sweaty and my knees are shaking.

But it's showtime!

Deep breath. Deep breath.

I remind myself of what I said to Ellie. It's about taking

risks. Putting yourself out there. Finding out what you can achieve. And having a good time.

The music begins. I raise my arms gracefully like I practiced. So far, so good. I bow my legs and move to the left when Twyla does. Then to the right. One arm comes down slowly, then the other.

Tiny little steps to the left. Tiny little steps to the right.

Arms up in a circle, then down.

I'm dancing ballet! Onstage! And I haven't knocked over anyone yet! Or fallen down!

I'm about to move to the right when I realize Twyla has moved to the left.

Oops. I'm only a beat behind, though. I quickly catch up.

I mess up one more time, when I spin the wrong way.

But then the music stops, and the curtain comes down. It's over!

When the curtain comes up again, the twelve dancing princesses of the Kingdom of Douze receive a standing ovation from the audience. Including King LaPear.

I curtsy along with the other sisters, sweaty and smiling.

I did it. I practiced, and I did it.

Is it possible I'm not that bad of a dancer after all?

*　　*　　*

After the performance, the princesses and I gather back-stage to change out of our ballet costumes. I slip on Ellie's pink uniform, white tights, and new black patent-leather shoes. Thankfully, everything fits me.

Ellie was right. King LaPear *didn't* notice that I was not his daughter.

How could he not notice? How could he not be watching closely, especially when his daughters dancing ballet is supposedly so important to him?

That doesn't seem right.

The king arrives backstage. I turn to face the wall, hoping he still won't notice I'm not Ellie.

"One, Two, Three, Four, Five, Six, Seven, Eight, Nine, Ten, Eleven, and Twelve," he calls out proudly. "Excellent performance!"

"Thank you, Father," Oona says.

"Meet me in the dining room for refreshments," the king adds. "It's time for Prince Gene to reveal where you go every night."

Oh, no. Oh, yes.

My heart races. I'm not ready for this.

The prince is going to be okay. Maryrose is going to be okay.

But the princesses are going to hate me.

We file out of the auditorium and head for the dining room.

I squeeze my eyes shut for a moment. I try not to think about how bad I feel for deceiving the princesses.

And I helped Ellie, didn't I? I feel a twinge of worry. I hope she and Jonah are okay. Shouldn't they be back by now?

In the dining room, Prince Gene is standing in front of the display case that holds the Ruby Crown.

He's smiling. And holding something behind his back.

The king's guests are crowded in the room as well, eager to watch the announcement. There are delicious chocolates and snacks laid out on the table.

The king, the princesses, and I line up facing Prince Gene.

Here we go.

The king lifts his chin. "All right, Prince Gene. You've had three nights to figure out what the princesses do to scuff their shoes. Are you able to tell me?"

The princesses all stare down at the floor. They really

look sad. Even Oona. I glance at Terry. I see a tear slipping down her cheek.

Aww.

"Yes, I *can* tell you," Prince Gene announces.

Terry's head jerks up in surprise.

The prince clears his throat. "The first two nights, the princesses put a sleeping potion in my drink to make me fall asleep," he says. "But last night, I saw everything!"

Several princesses gasp.

The king's eyes widen.

"Every night, the princesses sneak out of their room through a trapdoor and leave the castle through a secret exit," the prince continues, repeating what Jonah and I told him. "They take boats to an underground dance hall across the river. And dance the night away! That is why their shoes are scuffed and worn down every morning!"

The princesses' jaws drop. They begin muttering to one another.

I'm impressed that Prince Gene didn't get me and Jonah in trouble. He's sticking to the plan!

"Silence!" King LaPear bellows at the princesses. He turns to the prince. "All dancing other than ballet is illegal in Douze. Everyone knows that."

"Yes, that's why the dance hall is *secret*," the prince responds. "It's the Dance Resistance Party!"

The king narrows his eyes. He leans toward the prince. "What proof do you have of this?"

"This!" Prince Gene pulls out the silver goblet from behind his back. He holds it up so that the king can see the stamp reading DRP. "DRP! Dance Resistance Party! Get it?"

Oona gasps.

I bet she's thinking that having special goblets made for a secret dance party wasn't really a genius idea.

Terry's shoulders sag with relief. "Does this mean he's not getting his head chopped off?" she asks.

"It means," the king shouts, "that you're all in big trouble!"

Oh, no.

Oona glares at the prince. "How could you possibly know all this?" she demands. "You were asleep before we left last night. And asleep when we returned!"

"Aha!" the king shouts. "You admit it, One! You all sneak out!"

Oona's face falls. "Um, well. I . . ."

Terry steps forward. "How *did* you find out?" she asks Prince Gene. "There's no way you followed us. I would have seen you there! I was . . . I was looking for you," she admits, blushing.

I try to send Prince Gene a silent message. *Tell them about the invisibility cloak.* But Prince Gene can obviously only remember so much.

He looks around the room. His eyes land on me.

"There!" he says, pointing at me. "That girl — and her brother — told me everything and gave me the goblet! I did fall asleep after eating the ice cream, so they were the ones who saw what the princesses did."

Oh, no. I wish there was a trapdoor to disappear through right *here*.

"Abby and Jonah? The cooks?" Terry asks, looking confused.

Everyone turns to stare at me.

"Who are *you*?" the king demands, scowling at me. "Why are you in a princess uniform if you're a cook?"

"You're not really a cook?" Twyla asks me, looking sad.

CRUMBS.

Prince Gene clears his throat. "I don't know if she's a cook. But Abby and her brother want the crown ruby. I agreed to give it to them in exchange for the information and proof."

More gasps. More murmuring. My heart sinks. This is bad.

I hear footsteps. I look over at the door. It's Ellie, and Jonah is right behind her, the invisibility cloak covering part of his arm.

"There's the brother!" Prince Gene says, pointing at Jonah.

Jonah tries to put on the invisibility cloak but he gets tangled up in it, hopping and tripping in place. Only his feet are invisible.

"Oops," he says.

I cringe.

Ellie puts her hand on my shoulder. "Is what the prince says true?"

"Wait!" the king bellows. "I'm very confused," he adds, looking from me to his eleventh-born daughter. "Why are there *two* Elevens?"

I ignore the king and turn to Ellie. My stomach is churning. I could not feel worse.

"Yes," I admit to Ellie. "What the prince says is true. I'm sorry."

Everyone gasps again.

"How could you, Abby?" Ellie cries. "Oh, how could you?" She bursts into tears.

Oona shakes her head at me. She looks like my mom

does when I do something really, really wrong and she's really, really disappointed in me.

"We thought you were our friend!" Twyla says.

"Meanie!" Fanny and Franny say in unison.

"She's not a meanie!" Jonah says defensively. "She's a really nice big sister — well, ninety-nine percent of the time."

The king approaches me. "Ah, I see now. You're not Eleven. You're an impostor!"

His face is bright red and his hands are in fists. "Your crimes are: Impersonating a royal princess. Conspiring to steal the crown ruby. And being a meanie! Guards? Arrest her — and the brother! Throw them in the dungeon."

Oh, no. No, no, no! We can't be arrested and thrown in a dungeon. There's no time for that!

I need the crown ruby we were promised!

Two tall, burly guards come marching into the dining room.

One of them grabs me. The other grabs Jonah.

What now?

chapter thirteen

The Verdict

"Wait!" I call to the king before the guards drag us away. "Shouldn't we be rewarded for figuring out the mystery?"

The king hesitates. "Well . . . I guess. Perhaps I will take a year off your ten-year sentence."

Ten years? This king is really into severe punishments. At least he's not taking off our heads.

"No!" Terry cries. "You should add a year! Send her away for eleven! At least."

Gee, thanks, Terry.

"Don't you want to know why we did it?" I ask.

"You wanted the ruby," Terry says. "That's why. You're greedy!"

"No!" I say. "The ruby's not for us. There's a fairy named Maryrose and we're trying to help her. She sent us here for the ruby. It has healing properties. Minerta helped us and gave us the invisibility cloak."

"Minerta?" King LaPear says. "The old woman in the woods? She's a fairy?"

"Yes," I say.

"That might be useful," the king says, looking thoughtful. "Maybe Minerta would like to be the royal fairy."

"Perhaps," I say.

"Hmm. For alerting me to a kingdom fairy," King LaPear says, "I will take an extra year off your sentence. Now you're down to eight," he says, wagging his finger at me and Jonah.

I shake my head. "King LaPear, the only thing Jonah and I are *really* guilty of is helping the prince when we should have been helping the princesses."

"Well, you did both help me," Ellie says, stepping up. "Abby, you're a good dancer. And, Jonah, you're a good rower."

Me, a good dancer. Whodathunk?

Jonah's scrawny chest puffs out a bit.

The king stares at me. "What do you mean?" he asks. "Why should you have been helping the princesses? They need nothing!"

"King LaPear," I say, "your daughters, the royal princesses of Douze, are amazing young women. But you don't seem to see that."

"Yeah!" Jonah agrees. "They're all really cool!"

I see Oona's face light up. Ellie's eyes look teary.

"King LaPear," I continue, "each princess has her own personality and interests. Ellie is an excellent chess player. Terry is a gifted gymnast. Nina likes astronomy. Twyla is a great *tap* dancer. Eileen loves ballet, yes, but the others love different kinds of dance. I could go on and on. And I've only known your daughters a few days. They should have the freedom to follow their dreams. Not your dreams *for* them."

The king looks thoughtful for a moment, but then he waves his hand.

"I'm done listening!" he snaps. He turns to the guards. "Take this girl and boy to the dungeon at once!" He shakes his head. "Abby and Jonah," he mutters. "What weird names."

Terry steps forward. "Father. Abby is right. We lied to you and didn't tell you about where we went at night . . . because we felt we had no choice. You don't see us as we really are. We're so much more than perfect, prim ballet dancers. We're so much more than numbers."

The king taps a finger to his chin, thinking. "But Eleven put an impostor in her place. That was wrong! Where did you even go?"

"To a chess tournament. Father," Ellie says, "did you even notice I was gone?"

The king blushes. "Well, I, uh . . ."

While the king tries to think of a good defense for *that*, I turn to Ellie.

Not easy with a guard holding my arm tightly!

"Did you win the chess tournament, Ellie?" I ask.

If she won, that will definitely prove to the king that she's capable of so much more than he thinks.

"No," Ellie says. "I lost!"

Double crumbs.

"I lost," Ellie adds, smiling, "but it was challenging and

fun and I loved every minute of it. I came in fourth! Not bad for an Eleven, right?" She winks.

Jonah laughs. I don't shush him.

Ellie's sisters gather around to hug and high-five her.

"Congrats," Twyla says. "If you had more time to practice your chess skills, you'd be winning tournaments!"

The sisters turn to the king. He's gnawing on his lower lip. Rubbing his chin.

"I didn't even know Eleven *could* play chess," King LaPear says. "I think . . . that's wonderful!"

Ellie cheers. "Really? Yay! But, Father?"

"Yes?" he asks.

"I call myself Ellie, not Eleven. We all renamed ourselves."

One by one, the princesses tell the king the names they chose so that they're not just numbers. So that their names match how they feel inside. Interesting and smart and full of dreams and passions.

After the princesses are done, the king is silent. He gazes at the family portrait on the wall, deep in thought. Meanwhile, the guards hold on to me and Jonah, but they're seemingly waiting for the order from the king to actually take us away.

"I have a royal pronouncement," King LaPear finally says. We all hold our breath.

"The queen, your dear late mother," the king begins, "would be so proud of you princesses. She was like you — full of life and dreams. And she loved ballet." He nods at Eileen. "In retrospect, she and I probably shouldn't have named our daughters numbers, but we thought it would be easier to keep track of you that way." He shrugs. "I'm sorry."

"Thank you, Father," Oona says softly.

"When your mother passed away," the king goes on, "I was worried something would happen to one of you princesses. So I became protective. Too protective." The king gazes around at his daughters, some of whom are teary-eyed. The king looks choked up as well. I definitely have a lump in my throat. "In your mother's honor, in *your* honor, I will grant your wishes to use your new names and to follow your hearts. The law in Douze will change. Now all dancing will be permitted! You don't need to only dance ballet."

"Really?" Twyla cries.

"Really," says King LaPear.

The princesses clap and cheer. Some of them burst into happy tears.

King LaPear hugs his daughters one by one.

"Guards, release Abby and Jonah," the king orders.

Yay! The guards let go of our arms and step back.

Prince Gene clears his throat. "Um, excuse me, King LaPear. When do I become heir to the throne and get the Ruby Crown? I promised Abby I wouldn't force anyone to marry me, but I would still like the other stuff."

"You're not getting anything!" the king bellows at him. "You failed! Miserably! But as a changed man, I'm going to grant you clemency. One hundred years in prison instead of death."

Terry rushes forward. "Father, he did *try*. And there was a sleeping potion in his ice cream last night — we tricked him. So I think he should be free to go."

"Hmmm," the king says, thinking that over.

"Plus, I like him," Terry adds, blushing.

Yay! Go Terry for admitting her crush. That can be even harder than dancing in public.

The prince's chest puffs out. "Really? You like me?"

Terry smiles. "I do. You're kind. You're smart . . . in your own way," she adds.

I guess you could say that.

"All right, then," the king says. "If Three — I mean,

Terry believes in you, then so do I. No jail time for you, Prince Gene."

"Whew!" Prince Gene says, and takes Terry's hand. She grins.

Awww!

The king sighs. "So many changes. Well, here's another one. I'm getting old. And my firstborn, One — *Oona*," he corrects himself, "is now twenty-one. The same age her mother was when she became queen. In your mother's honor, I will plan to step down from my duties immediately, and you, Oona, will become the Queen of Douze."

The princesses gasp.

Oona is speechless, her hand over her heart. She's tearing up!

"Thank you, Father," she says at last. "I promise to be a good and fair queen."

"One moment," the king adds, and goes over to the display case. He reaches behind the case and presses something. A secret door slides open right in front of the crown.

What! Imagine how different this would have gone if Jonah and I had found that hidden button on our first morning here?

King LaPear gets up on a stepstool and takes out the

Ruby Crown. The big red ruby sparkles in the center, with twelve glittering diamonds surrounding it.

"This is now yours, Oona," the king says. "You will have a month of training on how to rule the kingdom, and then we shall hold your coronation ceremony."

He places the crown right on her head.

Amazingness! This went better than I even hoped!

"Father, as the crown princess of Douze," Oona begins, "I plan to hold dance parties every night."

"Fine, as long as I get an invitation," the king says, and does a little dance of his own.

The princesses all cheer.

"I would also like the princesses to do more activities outside the castle," Oona adds. "Like school, or gymnastics, or even ballet, for those who want to."

"I like that idea, too," the king says.

Yay!

"Abby, this is all thanks to you and your brother," Oona says, turning to me. "Is there anything I can do for you?"

"Yes!" I say. "We need that ruby." I point at the jewel on the crown. "To help our fairy friend Maryrose get her strength back."

"It's really nice how much you care about that fairy,"

Oona says. She takes off the crown, twists the ruby out of its setting, and hands it to me.

I stare at it. The big red ruby that will help heal Maryrose. I've got it!

But suddenly, I don't have it.

The ruby is snatched out of my hand!

My heart starts thumping. I turn around. There's no one even standing close to me. What the what?

I see the table move slightly and hear a male voice mutter, "Ow!"

I glance at Jonah's feet, which are still invisible. Is someone else wearing an invisibility cloak?

"Who are you?" I call out. "*Where* are you?"

"There's no one here," the same voice says. Then he adds, "Um, I didn't mean to say that."

Jonah is standing close to where the voice came from. He reaches out and grabs the air, and suddenly, an invisibility cloak slides off an older man in a soldier's uniform. He has gray hair and a gray beard and is kind of weary-looking, like he came from the battlefield.

"Who are you?" the king yells.

"Just a soldier who wants more," the man says. And then he yanks the cloak back over himself and disappears again.

chapter fourteen

Find That Ruby

a soldier.
Suddenly, the original story comes back to me. The final person to solve the mystery of where the princesses went every night was an old soldier! He's the one Minerta was supposed to give the invisibility cloak to, and he was the one who was supposed to spy on the sisters and marry the oldest princess. Prince Gene must have been the last person to try to win the contest before this soldier.

"Wait!" I cry. "I know who you are! You were going to try to win the contest! You went to see Minerta, didn't you? And she gave you an invisibility cloak!"

"Yeah, and I would have won if you two hadn't helped *him*!" I hear the soldier's voice call out from across the room.

"I guess Minerta made more invisibility cloaks after all," Jonah says.

Just then, the crown is yanked from Oona's hand and disappears.

"Oh, no!" Oona screams. "He has the crown!"

"Guards! Find that soldier!" the king bellows.

"How can we find him if we can't see him?" one of the guards responds.

Everyone in the room — guards, princesses, guests — starts reaching in front of them, trying to grab the thief that they can't see. It looks kind of like a dance recital, actually. A chaotic one.

A woman screams, "Someone stole my purse!"

A man screams, "Someone stole my wallet!"

A kid screams, "Someone stole my lollipop! I was licking it!"

What is wrong with this soldier? Taking a lollipop someone else was LICKING? That's just gross.

"You can't stop me if you can't see me," the soldier's voice cackles from one side of the room. "So much good stuff in here, and it's all going to be mine, mine, mine! I deserve it all! Even the lollipop!"

The voice keeps moving around the room. As soon as I think it's in one area, I hear him in another. If only we could see him.

Suddenly, I have an idea. "Jonah, give me our cloak!"

Jonah picks up the cloak from his feet and tosses it to me. "Here! Why?"

I throw it over my head. "Because I can see myself when I'm under it. So maybe I can see the soldier, too!"

I spin around, and there he is! It worked! The soldier is holding a giant bag that's bursting with stuff, and he's trying to climb out the window.

"He's right there!" I point.

"We can't see where you're pointing," Jonah says. "You're invisible!"

"By the second window!" I say.

The guards start to run over, but Terry's one step ahead of them. Literally. She does a perfect flying leap through the air and lands right by the second window. Wowza. I wonder if Douze has an Olympic team. She could take home gold for gymnastics.

Terry yanks off the soldier's invisibility cloak.

The soldier tumbles to the ground, the bag of stolen goods skittering out of his hand. The guards immediately rush over and grab him.

"That was amazing!" Prince Gene tells Terry. She beams.

Oona picks up the bag of stolen goods and starts returning things to people.

"Curse you all!" the soldier sputters.

Oona frowns, glancing back at the soldier. "If Abby and Jonah hadn't come along, one of us would have had to marry this jerk?" she asks.

"Yup," I say. "And I know for a fact it was going to be you."

She shivers. "Whew. Thank you."

"No problem," I say.

"Here you go," Oona says, placing the ruby back in my hand. "I hope it helps your friend."

"Me too," I say, holding it tight.

The last item Oona takes from the bag is the crown. She puts it on her head. "Guards," she says regally. "Please take this soldier away. It's my time to rule."

Time.

Oh, no!

I glance at my watch. It's 6:59 in the morning back home.

"Come on, Jonah," I say. "We have to find the portal now!"

"Can we say good-bye first?" Jonah asks.

And so we do. We hug every single princess good-bye. We even hug Prince Gene and King LaPear.

I give extra hugs to Ellie, Twyla, and Terry. I'm going to miss them.

"Where's the portal, Abby?" Jonah asks, looking around. "Maybe it's that platter of cookies," he suggests, pointing to the buffet.

It would be fun to jump into a platter of chocolate chip cookies and eat a few on the way back to Smithville. But unlikely.

Still. I knock on the platter three times. Nothing. I take a few cookies to go, anyway.

"Maybe that huge clock in the hallway?" I suggest.

We run out of the dining room and over to the clock.

We knock. Nothing.

And suddenly, I know.

"Jonah!" I cry. "The trapdoor!"

His eyes light up. "Yeah! I bet it's that."

I go running down the hall. And stop when I realize Jonah isn't following me.

I turn around. "Jonah! Come on!"

He frowns. "What if when we get home, Prince has forgotten me? What if he's decided he wants to be Maryrose's dog forever?"

I walk up to Jonah. "Prince is our dog," I assure him again. "He may like Maryrose, but he won't leave you. I'm sure of it."

"I hope not," he says.

"Come on!" I say, and start running again.

This time Jonah follows. Whew.

In the princesses' bedroom, I knock on the trapdoor three times.

I see the sides of the trapdoor start glowing purple. I was right!

I'm about to open the door when I realize something — I'm still wearing the pink princess uniform.

Just then, Ellie and Twyla walk into the bedroom.

"Ellie!" I cry, relieved. "Do you know where my clothes are? The hoodie and T-shirt and jeans I was wearing last night?"

Ellie frowns. "Probably in our closet," she says. She hurries to the closet and peeks inside. "Oof, I don't see your clothes, Abby. It's a mess in here."

"We don't have time!" Jonah tells me worriedly.

"Here, take these," Ellie says, tossing me the outfit she wore to the dance party our first night — the red tunic and striped leggings. "I have plenty of other outfits. And you can keep my uniform, too. I won't need to wear it anymore."

"Thank you, Ellie!" I cry. Hopefully she or one of the other princesses can get good use out of my hoodie, T-shirt, and jeans.

"Bye!" Ellie and Twyla call.

I fling open the door. The steps are a swirling purple haze.

Smithville, Maryrose, and Prince — here we come!

I take Jonah's hand and down we go.

chapter fifteen

This Might Be Useful

t *HUMP.*

We land in our basement on our bottoms. We're home.

I take a quick look at the mirror. It's still cracked. What does that mean for Maryrose? I hope she's okay.

I glance at my watch. "It's after seven! Dad must be up already. What do we do?"

"I got this," Jonah says.

I turn to the sound of his voice. But I don't see him anywhere. "Jonah?"

Only his head is suddenly visible. "Yes?" he says with a grin.

"You took the invisibility cloak!"

"I did!"

"But we aren't supposed to take things from fairy tales!"

"We took Prince that time!" he argues. "And you took Ellie's clothes."

"But . . ."

"Why don't we use it to sneak upstairs and argue about this later?"

He has a point. He pulls the cloak over us, and together we rush up the stairs to the first floor. I peek around the corner. I can see my dad in the kitchen, pouring orange juice into four glasses. When he glances over his shoulder, we freeze.

But he can't see us. Whew!

Silently, we hurry up the second flight of stairs to my bedroom.

We race inside and take off the cloak.

Prince is curled up on my bed. When he sees us, he jumps up, wagging his tail. Jonah rushes over and Prince greets him with licks and doggie kisses.

Awww.

"You did miss me!" Jonah says, all smiles.

Woof! Prince barks.

I reach over and scratch behind his ears. He sighs happily. He missed me, too.

I look around my room. No sign of Maryrose.

"Maryrose!" I call. "We're back!"

No response.

I bite my lip and turn to Jonah. He looks worried, too.

I run over to my jewelry box and open the lid. There she is! She's tiny and lying down, and flickering in and out. She looks very tired.

"I'm so . . . glad . . . you're back," she says in a faint voice. "I didn't have . . . the strength . . . to open the lid."

Poor Maryrose!

I pull the ruby from my pocket. I put it beside her in the jewelry box.

"We got the crown ruby," I tell her proudly.

She puts her hand on the ruby. It sparkles and shines.

And then *Maryrose* sparkles and shines. And then shines brighter. And brighter. And then she's suddenly sitting on my bed. Full-sized. And most importantly, not flickering in and out.

"I feel so much better!" Maryrose cries. "I'm not at full strength yet. But the more I touch the ruby, the stronger I'll get."

"Yay!" I say.

"You did it, Abby and Jonah!" Maryrose exclaims. "You are amazing. Thank you so much."

"You're welcome," I say, blushing. "It wasn't too hard." I get an idea. "Jonah has something for you, too."

"I do?" Jonah asks, looking up from his happy reunion with Prince.

"Yes! The invisibility cloak!"

"Oh." Jonah frowns a little. "That's for me, not for her."

"Jonah!"

"Fine," he grumbles, handing it over to Maryrose. Then his eyes light up. "But can I borrow it? Just once or twice? Like on Halloween?"

"Of course," Maryrose says. "Thank you. This will help me get stronger, too. Being invisible lets me store up my energy."

"Um, Maryrose?" Jonah says. "When you're strong enough to leave, are you going to take Prince with you?"

"Of course not!" she responds. "He's been wonderful and kept me great company, but Prince is your dog. And it's clear he loves you and your sister very much."

Woof! Prince agrees.

"Awesome," Jonah says. He looks very relieved. To be honest, I'm relieved, too. I'd be so sad without Prince.

"So what happens now?" I ask Maryrose. "Are you strong enough to go home? Where is home?"

"Well, first I'm going to rest up in the jewelry box and keep my hand on the ruby," Maryrose says as she puts on the invisibility cloak. "And then we'll talk."

Just like that, she's gone.

"Guess I was a worrywart for nothing," Jonah comments, cuddling Prince in his lap.

I grin. "I get that way, too."

I really do. I'm going to work at not worrying so much. Sure, sometimes things can go wrong. Like with THE INCIDENT. But sometimes things go right. Like with the ballet recital.

And you've got to aim and hope for things to go right, right? Right.

"I'm going to ask Mom and Dad for a chess set," Jonah says.

"You are?"

"Yup. Watching Ellie was fun. I want to learn how to play."

I smile. "Then you can teach me."

Jonah runs downstairs with Prince on his heels.

I go over to my jewelry box, which my nana gave me a long time ago. It's decorated with characters from fairy tales. There's Cinderella and Sleeping Beauty and Jack from *Jack and the Beanstalk*. Every time Jonah and I come back from a fairy tale, the characters on the jewelry box change to match how we messed up the story. Or made it better.

I turn the box gently, not wanting to disturb Maryrose inside.

And there they are!

The twelve dancing princesses. They're on the castle grounds, and each one is doing her own thing and wearing her own clothes. Oona has on her crown, and there's an emerald where the ruby used to be. Terry is doing a cartwheel, Prince Gene smiling beside her. Ellie is playing chess, and oh! She's wearing my jeans and hoodie. Twyla is tap dancing. Eileen is in her tutu and ballet slippers. And sitting on a blanket nearby, smiling proudly, is the king.

I already miss the princesses. I miss the castle. The donuts.

I even miss the dance parties.

Although tonight, I have a dance party of my own.

Yup.

Before I went through the mirror into Douze, I wasn't planning to go to the school dance at all.

But now . . . well, now I'm kind of looking forward to it.

I arrive at the school dance, my stomach full of butterflies. Streamers and colorful balloons are everywhere. It's not as fancy as the DRP but still has a festive feeling. There's even a disco ball. It's hanging from the basketball net, and it's making light flicker on the walls.

Everyone from the fifth grade is here. I wave at Frankie and Robin, and they rush over to me. Frankie is in her jeans with the checkered back pockets. Robin is wearing her off-the-shoulder sweater. And I'm wearing Ellie's outfit — the red tunic with striped leggings.

"You came!" Frankie says. "We were worried you'd be too busy with your guest."

"I came," I say. And I'm glad I did.

Penny hurries over in her gold dress and new shoes.

"I like your outfit, Abby," she tells me, sounding impressed.

A song we all love comes on. Robin and Penny run out to the dance floor. Frankie grabs my hand, pulling me along.

I freeze. I can't help it.

There's a part of me that wants to say no. That's still scared of repeating THE INCIDENT.

But then I remember how fun it was dancing at the DRP. How I let go and stopped worrying about the steps, or what other people were thinking.

Who cares if one mean person, one time, thought I wasn't a good dancer? Everyone at the ballet recital thought I did a good job. No one threw rotten tomatoes at me, did they?

No.

The truth is, not everyone has to like the way I dance.

The only person who has to like the way I dance is . . . me.

So I join Frankie, Robin, and Penny on the dance floor. I move to the music, shake my hips, and clap my hands. I remind myself — no one is even watching! Everyone is just doing their own thing.

And I'm having fun. That's what matters, right?

As I spin around, I see a red sparkle to my left.

A red sparkle that isn't from the disco ball.

I stop. I look.

Was that the ruby?

No, couldn't be.

But then I hear, "Looking good."

I know that voice.

It's Maryrose! Under the invisibility cloak!

"What are you doing here?" I ask.

"Looking for something," she says.

"At my school? What?"

"I'll tell you more tomorrow," she says. "Right now, just have fun."

"Do you need my help?"

"I will soon," she says. "And you know . . . if you ever need my help, I'm here for you, too. I'll always appreciate what you've done for me, Abby."

"Anytime," I say, choked up.

"Who are you talking to?" Frankie asks.

"Um, no one," I say quickly, clearing my throat. I do a twirl so she doesn't see the emotion on my face. "Just singing along!"

And I do. I dance and sing with my friends, knowing that they'll be my friends no matter what. Even if I dance badly or knock over a cake.

But it feels good to know that there's a fairy nearby, in case I need some extra help, too.

Get lost in an extra-special adventure with Abby . . .

Look for:

Whatever After Special edition #3
ABBY in NEVERLAND

acknowledgments

Thank you!

The Scholastic team: Aimee Friedman, Taylan Salvati, Lauren Donovan, Rachel Feld, Erin Berger, Olivia Valcarce, Melissa Schirmer, Elizabeth Parisi, Abby McAden, David Levithan, Lizette Serrano, Emily Heddleson, Sue Flynn, and everyone in Sales and in the School Channels.

As always, my amazing agent, Laura Dail. Hollywood friends, Austin Denesuk, Matthew Snyder, Berni Barta, Rachel and Terry Winter, and Jennilee Cummings. Extra thanks to Lauren Walters.

All my friends, family, writing buddies, and first readers: Bonnie Altro, Elissa Ambrose, Robert Ambrose, the Bilermans, Max Brallier, Julie Buxbaum, Jess Braun, Rose Brock, Jeremy Cammy, Julia DeVillers, Elizabeth Eulberg, Stuart Gibbs, Karina Yan Glaser, Adele Griffin, Brooke Hecker, Robin Hoffman, Emily Jenkins, Lauren Kisilevsky, Gordon Korman, Leslie Margolis, the Mittlemans, Aviva Mlynowski, Larry Mlynowski, Lauren Myracle, Zibby Owens, James Ponti, Melissa Posten, Melissa Senate, Rebecca

Serle, Courtney Sheinmel, Jennifer E. Smith, Christina Soontornvat, the Steins, the Swidlers, Louisa Weiss, and the Wolfes.

Thanks and love to Todd and to my two little princesses, Chloe and Anabelle. Hugs and wishes to my Whatever After readers. May every day include a dance party.

Read all the Whatever After books!

Whatever After #1: FAIREST of ALL

In their first adventure, Abby and Jonah wind up in the story of Snow White. But when they stop Snow from eating the poisoned apple, they realize they've messed up the whole story! Can they fix it — and still find Snow her happy ending?

Whatever After #2: IF the SHOE FITS

This time, Abby and Jonah find themselves in Cinderella's story. When Cinderella breaks her foot, the glass slipper won't fit! With a little bit of magic, quick thinking, and luck, can Abby and her brother save the day?

Whatever After #3: SINK or SWIM

Abby and Jonah are pulled into the tale of *The Little Mermaid* — a story with an ending that is *not* happy. So Abby and Jonah mess it up on purpose! Can they convince the mermaid to keep her tail before it's too late?

Whatever After #4: DREAM ON

Abby and Jonah are lost in Sleeping Beauty's story, along with Abby's friend Robin. Before they know it, Sleeping Beauty is wide awake and Robin is fast asleep. How will Abby and Jonah make things right?

Whatever After #5: BAD HAIR DAY

When Abby and Jonah fall into Rapunzel's story, they mess everything up by giving Rapunzel a haircut! Can they untangle this fairy tale disaster in time?

Whatever After #6: COLD as ICE

When their dog, Prince, runs through the mirror, Abby and Jonah have no choice but to follow him into the story of the Snow Queen. It's a winter wonderland . . . but the Snow Queen is mean, and she FREEZES Prince! Can Abby and Jonah save their dog . . . and themselves?

Whatever After #7: BEAUTY QUEEN

Abby and Jonah fall into the story of *Beauty and the Beast*. When Jonah is the one taken prisoner instead of Beauty, Abby has to find a way to fix this fairy tale . . . before things get pretty ugly!

Whatever After #8: ONCE upon a FROG

When Abby and Jonah fall into the story of *The Frog Prince*, they realize the princess is so rude they don't even *want* her help! But will they be able to figure out how to turn the frog back into a prince all by themselves?

Whatever After #9: GENIE in a BOTTLE

The mirror has dropped Abby and Jonah into the story of *Aladdin*! But when things go wrong with the genie, the siblings have to escape an enchanted cave, learn to fly a magic carpet, and figure out WHAT to wish for . . . so they can help Aladdin and get back home!

Whatever After #10: SUGAR and SPICE

When Abby and Jonah fall into *Hansel and Gretel*, they can't wait to see the witch's cake house (yum). But they didn't count on the witch trapping them there! Can they escape and make it back to home sweet home?

Whatever After #11: TWO PEAS in a POD

When Abby lands in *The Princess and the Pea*—and has trouble falling asleep on a giant stack of mattresses—everyone in the kingdom thinks SHE is the princess they've all been waiting for. Though Abby loves the royal treatment, she and Jonah need to find a real princess to rule the kingdom . . . and get back home in time!

Whatever After #12: SEEING RED

My, what big trouble we're in! When Abby and Jonah fall into *Little Red Riding Hood*, they're determined to save Little Red and her grandma from being eaten by the big, bad wolf. But there's quite a surprise in store when the siblings arrive at Little Red's grandma's house.

Whatever After #13: SPILL the BEANS

Abby and Jonah FINALLY land in the story of *Jack and the Beanstalk*! But when they end up with the magic beans, can they get Jack out of his gigantic troubles?

Whatever After #14: GOOD as GOLD

In the story of *Goldilocks and the Three Bears*, there's porridge to sample and beds to test out! But if Abby and Jonah help Goldilocks, will they run into trouble with the Bear family?

Whatever After Special edition #1: ABBY in WONDERLAND

In this Special Edition, Abby and three of her friends fall down a rabbit hole into *Alice's Adventures in Wonderland*! They meet the Mad Hatter, the caterpillar, and Alice herself... but only solving a riddle from the Cheshire Cat can help them escape the terrible Queen of Hearts. Includes magical games and an interview with the author!

Whatever After Special edition #2:
ABBY in OZ

Abby's not in Smithville anymore! In this extra-enchanting second Special Edition, Abby and her friends are off on a new adventure inside *The Wonderful Wizard of Oz*. Can they find the courage, brains, and heart — along with a whole cast of new friends — and make their way back home? Includes bonus games and activities.

about the author

Sarah Mlynowski is the *New York Times* and *USA Today* best-selling author of the Whatever After series, the Magic in Manhattan series, and a bunch of other books for teens, tweens, and grown-ups, including the Upside-Down Magic series, which she cowrites with Lauren Myracle and Emily Jenkins, and which was adapted into a movie for the Disney Channel. Originally from Montreal, Sarah now lives in Los Angeles with her family. Visit her online at sarahm.com and find her on Instagram, Facebook, and Twitter at @sarahmlynowski.

And don't miss:

BEST WISHES

A magical new series
created by Sarah Mlynowski!